Nicholas E Watkins

JADE

Nicholas E Watkins

Other Tim Burr Thrillers by Nicholas E Watkins

Tanker

Bank

Dealer

Oligarch

Steel

Hack

About the Author

Nicholas Watkins lives on the coast with his wife and has four children He is a retired Accountant and has a Degree in Economics. He worked in the City of London for many years.

Jade

Copyright © Nicholas E Watkins 2018

The right of Nicholas E Watkins to be identified as the Author of the Work has been asserted by him in accordance with the Copyright, Designs and patent Act 1988.

All characters in this publication are fictional and any resemblance to real persons living or dead is purely coincidental.

Chapter 1

2007

The traffic had cleared on Commercial Road in the East End of London. The commute home from the City had started early as it always does on a Friday. The City would now be a virtual graveyard for the weekend until the millions streamed into work once again on Monday morning.

The bars would still be packed with drinkers. The bankers, stock traders and financial service elite would perhaps be having their drinks in the high end City clubs, bars or restaurants before heading to the West End. The more trendy young would be in the overpriced bars in Aldgate. They all were just over a mile in distance from where the Mosque was situated but a million miles away in terms of life style and wealth.

The inside of the Transit Van was becoming hot and stuffy despite the coolness of the evening air outside. The sound of the rain drumming on the metal roof was incessant and the occupants perspired as they sat in the cramped interior.

There were eight vans parked in the area. They had gradually moved into place one by one so avoiding drawing attention to themselves. On the streets surrounding the area, further armed officers loitered in plain clothes. All were in constant communication with Command and Control.

SO15 or Counter Terrorism Command had come into being just two years earlier with the merger of Special Branch or SO12 and the Anti-Terrorist Branch, SO13. Part of the London Metropolitan Police, it shared its home with the National Terrorism Policing Network. With over one and a half thousand police officers, it worked with the other agencies MI5 and MI6 to combat all forms of terrorist threats.

Months of hard work gathering intelligence, surveillance and monitoring of communications had brought about this night's coordinated operation. Every detail had been meticulously planned and the highly trained personnel were set to execute the operation.

Suzy Webb felt nervous. This was her first full scale operation. She had been through the rigorous training that all SO15 officers were subjected to, along with the psychological profiling that accompanied it. Still she felt apprehensive. Until you were faced with the real thing you could never be sure how you would react.

The silence in the back of the vehicle was oppressive and the wait nerve jangling. She was feeling the tension and her stomach was filled with butterflies. She doubled checked her equipment. She felt the adrenaline sharpening her awareness. One of her colleagues gave her a reassuring smile.

He was called Charles and they had gone through the academy together. He was tall, handsome and confident. He had been in the military prior to joining the Force. He had faced combat and, unlike Suzy, held no doubt as to his ability to perform under fire.

She knew he was attracted to her. She was thirty two, with big brown eyes, an olive complexion and long black hair. Her grand mother had been Indian, an immigrant to the UK who had married an Englishman. Two generations had resulted in Suzy.

He had asked her out during training on several occasions. He was thirty six and his marriage had disintegrated as so many military marriages did. The separation and danger of military operations many miles from home inevitably put a strain on any relationship. Charles's marriage came to end while he was in Afghanistan. He received his 'Dear John letter' three weeks into his second tour.

With hindsight, all the signs were there when he was home on leave. The sparkle had gone from her. There was an air of secrecy and vagueness about his wife. She spent long periods out of the home, visiting friends or working late. He saw the clues but chose to ignore them.

Her letter still came as a shock. Her new man was one of his friends. He knew of course that he had a thing for his wife. They had joked about it. With Charles away he had become closer to her. He was there to help when she was lonely. Charles understood but it still hurt.

That was in the past. Nearly three years in the past. Life moves on. He had moved on. He looked across at Suzy and gave her the thumbs up sign. She smiled nervously back at him.

He had been smitten with her from the first. He had moved away from Stockport to London when he left the Army. The town was large but not large enough to avoid seeing his wife and her new lover. He needed a clean break so he transferred to the Met.

He and Suzy got along well and he felt there was a connection. He thought that something might come of it but somehow nothing did. There was a barrier that he just could not identify. The spark never quite ignited between them. He still remained hopeful that something would change.

Suzy smiled back at him. She knew how he felt. She just did not want a man. She had a woman in her life. She wanted to tell him that she really liked him but not in the way he wished. She was not keen on facing the repercussions of coming out. She knew full well that as soon as she admitted to her homosexuality she would always be know as that lezzy cop or the dyke. One thing you could always count on in the Force was a good dose or sexism and racism. It was part of the culture, no matter the efforts put in to combat it.

Suddenly it was action. The order had been issued to go. The doors to the vehicles slammed open and the streets around the Mosque were filled with police running and shouting warnings. Marked police cars with blue lights flashing appeared and blocked all roads into and out of the area. The Mosque was isolated and contained as SO15 moved in.

The men were at prayers and all exits were blocked. The worshippers would be processed and identified as they left. They were not the primary target. Intelligence had identified the meeting and classrooms that were accessed through doors next to the Mosque. The Mosque had not been purpose built and was in what had been a commercial building. In years gone by it had been a garment factory with a large shop floor that now accommodated the Prayer Hall.

The raid had been prompted by information that one of the rooms was being used by a radical group aiming to bomb a high profile target in central London. Somewhere in the maze of rooms there was bomb making equipment and the bombers. Tonight was the eve of the suspected attack on the Capital.

"Armed police, armed police," the shouts went out as they poured into the building. The officers made as much noise as they could, hoping to disorientate the occupants and impose their dominance.

"Up, follow me," shouted Charles as he ran up the stairs.

Suzy's heart was pounding with the rush of adrenaline. "Go, go," she shouted.

The building was a maze of corridors and smaller and larger rooms. Some of the rooms were used as Madrasas, Islamic schools for the women and children, others for meeting and administration.

"I have lost my bearings" screamed Charlie. It was clear that the building had been extensively modified internally and bore no resemblance to the plans held at the Local Planning Office.

"Keep going," Suzy responded.

Police were running in all directions. They had rehearsed every detail of the raid but that was now all to no avail. The building had obviously been extended into the adjacent building, the Mosque. It now linked to floors above the prayer hall that were not there on paper. The area was twice what had been expected. To sweep it they were forced to split up. There were not enough officers for the size of the theatre of operation that they now found themselves in.

It was chaotic, panicked, confused and rapidly becoming less and less coordinated. Suzy lost sight of Charles and her fellow officers and found herself in a corridor facing a large heavy door. She was isolated and disorientated.

She was out of breath and breathing heavily. The door was clearly sound proof. She stopped and hesitated. She knew she should shout the warning, "Armed police," but she didn't. How could she? She did not know what awaited her on the other side of the door. For all she knew it was a group of heavily armed Jihadis. She reasoned that the door was sound proof and they would not be aware of her presence. She had at least the element of surprise on her side even if she had no backup.

She took a deep breath and launched herself at the door. It flew back and she ran into the room shouting "armed police don't move." She was dazzled. The corridor had been devoid of lighting and she had been reliant on the torch affixed to her shoulder.

There was a loud bang to her left and from the limit of her peripheral vision restricted by her helmet, she sensed movement. Instinctively she spun to face the threat. She fired.

The room filled with sound of screaming. Her eyes gradually adjusted to the brightness. The room was full of women and children. They were holding some form of party. There were balloons, gifts, cakes and sweets. She focused on the direction of her burst of gunfire.

A young woman lay on the floor. Her face was no more. The three bullets Suzy fired had all hit there target and were neatly grouped. They had completely destroyed the woman's features. All that was left was more akin to a pile of butcher's offal than a face. Brains, blood, flesh and bone had exploded across the floor. She lay dead in an expanding pool of her own blood.

Suzy stood uncomprehending at the scene. It was all wrong. She had heard the sound of shot. She had seen a flash. While the remaining women lay huddled, shielding their children she made her way to the corpse of the young woman.

She forced herself to look at the body. There was no sign of a gun or a weapon of any kind on or near the body. How could that be? She had been so sure.

She bent down and studied the body. Across her chest were the remains of confetti and thin paper streamers. She looked at her hand. The realisation of what had occurred slowly sank in. In her hand was the round small container of the party popper.

She had entered the room with no warning just as the young woman had pulled the string that fires the streamers into the air. No guns, no bombs, no Jihadis, just a group of women and children celebrating the dead girls upcoming wedding, an engagement party.

"Clear?" It was Charles. He had eventually caught up.

He surveyed the scene. For an instant he was paralysed. He recovered and his training took over. "Out, clear the area." he ordered.

The women, cowering, moved passed him as he stood in the doorway. They held their children close as they passed and moved along the corridors to the exit and the waiting officers.

Suzy responded to the prompting in her headset. The sound of the shooting had been picked up by the Officer in charge of the operation in the Counter Terrorism control room.

"I have shot someone," said Suzy.

It was clear from her voice that all was not well. "Switch channels. Say nothing until you do." Charles received a communication and left to escort the women from the premises leaving Suzy alone with the dead woman.

"Tell me," said the voice in her ear.

She explained the sequence of events that had led to the shooting. As she spoke she realised she had no way out. She had entered a room with no warning and shot someone. She knew at best it would be a man slaughter charge.

"Listen to me and do exactly as I tell you. Leave the room and guard the entrance. Do not let anyone in. I have issued instructions that no one is to enter and disturb the scene. Are you listening?"

"Yes" Suzy answered, her voice shaking.

"Let no one enter. I will be there in fifteen minutes and I shall take charge personally on the ground. Stay calm. It will be alright, trust me."

Chapter 2

Today

He was careful to keep his hoody drawn tight over his head and face as he left Luton railway station. He knew that CCTV was always there watching and capturing everything. It was hard to go anywhere in England without being caught by the cameras. The cameras at this very station had captured the his Jihadi brothers as they set off to bomb the Capital in 2005.

Mo, not his real name, made his way past the sports centre and more cameras to the older part of town. He paused to check the route on his phone. He located the street name sign and made his way to the number. He did not stand out in this predominantly Asian area and there were no cameras to watch him at this location in any event.

The house he was looking for was a terrace that had been divided up into flats. He rang the bell for the ground floor apartment. He saw the curtains move before the buzzer went, allowing him to open the exterior door and enter.

The interior hallway was drab, dirty and had seen better days. It was typical student accommodation, tatty but affordable. The door to the flat opened and without a word he entered. The occupants were expecting him.

"As-Salaam-Alaikum." Peace be unto you.

"Wa-Alaikum-Salaam," And unto you peace, the greetings were

exchanged.

Mo settled on the sofa and the three occupants sat around him. "The time my brothers, is nearly upon us. In the next few days you will receive details of the target."

There three men were tense. Things had just become real. Their commitment was undeniable but the translating of thought into action was never easy. Doubts were inevitable. Fear was now part of the equation. They were committed but still they were human with human weaknesses.

"Come brothers, less anxiety. This is what we have been waiting for. You will be forever honoured. You will earn your place directly in paradise."

One of the men found his voice, "the equipment and the funding?"

"In hand, you will have all you need."

Mo left feeling reassured that they were to be relied on. The walk back to the station saw him in time to get the next train. He has many such journeys to make. In the next few weeks he would be coordinating cells across the whole Country.

As the train made its way along the tracks he amused himself by reading the latest tweets. He smiled as he read the one from US President, launching a scathing attack, claiming Pakistan "gives safe haven to the terrorists we hunt" and thinks "of our leaders as fools". He knew that the US was considering denying Islamabad $255 million in aid in a show of discontent with its efforts to fight terrorism.

"We can mange without your money," he said under his breath.

The Eastern Regional office of MI5 had been set up after the London bombing and had been in operation for over eight years. MI5 had been slow at first to respond to the Islamic threat produced by home grown terrorists but they had learned lessons. Staff had been rapidly recruited and operations expanded. The number of watchers on the ground had dramatically expanded. Not everyone on the Agency's radar could be put under surveillance all the time. There were just too many but with careful coordination across the various other agencies including the Police Counter Terrorism units and GCHQ, the UK's ears and electronic surveillance HQ, the rate of threat detection was increasingly becoming more effective.

Mo has not been on anyone's radar up until that morning. He may have avoided CCTV but he had not avoided the MI5 watchers of the house in Luton that he visited. The three men of Pakistani origin who lived in the flat had managed to draw their attention earlier.

They were considered a real and credible threat. Initially, GCHQ had picked upon some traffic between the occupants of the house and a few radical internet sites linked to ISIS, the Islamic Terrorist organisation committed to restoring a Caliphate in the Middle East. They had been monitored but not investigated.

Things had changed when encryption had been used to exchange emails from their accounts. It was a red flag. Most people do not encrypt to order a pizza or send a birthday greeting. Big business needs to protect its data but students usually have nothing of value to protect. As the frequency of the communications increased so did the interest of the Security Service. The watchers had been assigned to watch the student flat in Luton.

Mo's arrival at the house had been observed and photographs had been taken. MI5 had expanded its recruitment to now include a more ethnic mix, including Pakistanis and Indians. In the past it had been focused on the IRA, the Irish terrorists who were seeking reunification of the North and the South of Ireland. The Good Friday Peace Agreement had substantially reduced that threat but in its place, the Jihadis had risen to the fore along with the GRU, the Russian secret service, as the new threats.

"Do we know this guy?" The head of MI5's regional office asked as Mo's pictures came through from their field agents. Facial recognition software was employed and databases searched. The answer was no.

He made a decision. "Follow him."

It was a risk pulling the surveillance from the suspect house in Luton. It could go badly wrong. There was nothing at this stage to identify Mo as any sort of security threat. He had only been a visitor at a suspect address and even the occupants of the flat were not considered high risk.

It was a judgement call made by the regional commander. He was aware of the outcomes, good and bad. By pulling the watchers off the flat's residents he ran the risk of them being free to carry out any activity without hindrance. If they left loaded with a bag of high explosive and set it off in Central London he knew the price in lives would be catastrophic and the damage to MI5 reputation and credibility equally devastating.

He made the call and it turned out to be the right one. Twenty four hours later the reports were in on their new Person of Interest.

After his activity on the first day of surveillance, more resources had been added. Now there were eight agents trailing him round the clock. Phones, tablets and his computers were being watched. Every move, contact and location was being recorded. As the data was studied the picture cleared.

They did not know what the threat was but they did know it was serious and imminent. Over a three day period he had visited addresses all over the Country, eight in all. Five of them were already on the MI5 radar. All eight now were under round the clock electronic and physical watch. Red flags were waving and alarm bells were ringing.

Chapter 3

He awoke to the sound of his alarm. It was a new day and the Sun's rays were already peeping through the gap in the curtains. His head cleared and he let out a breath before sitting up. Only he did not sit up.

Anthony Burr was confused momentarily. What was happening? What was wrong with him? Why did his body not obey him? He lay in the semi darkness of his bedroom panicking at his paralysis.

Clarity came as the last vestige of sleep left him. In the comfort of his bed and the oblivion of sleep, he had forgotten. He had forgotten the reality. He had forgotten how he had come to this.

The detail would never return. He had the memory of the moments immediately before and then the memory of waking in the hospital. He saw himself as if from a third person perspective enter the barn. He saw Harriet Shaw, stripped naked, tied down then pain and darkness.

Anthony, Tim as he was known to all, had been rushed into hospital. The trauma to his head was serious and his brain had begun to swell. He had been placed in an induced coma for weeks. The prognosis had been slow but gradually he had improved.

He eventually came to. There at the side of the bed was Harriet Shaw. She had sat beside his bed day in and day out. Never doubting, constantly hoping and willing him to recover. She was eventually rewarded when his eyes opened.

He tried to speak. He had opened his mouth and just a groan

16

emerged. "Where am I?"

Over the next few days he was assessed. It became apparent that all was not well. There had been a bleed to the brain. His hearing and speech were fine but that was not the case with his movement. His left side was partially paralysed.

Depression was the true enemy though. He could not move his left arm and his left leg properly. He felt that his life was over, that he was now consigned to a wheelchair. Even though only in his forties, he felt that his was no longer whole. The worm of despondency began to gnaw at his mind. He did not want to live like this.

His mind took him to the dark place where resilience can give way to apathy. He did not want to live like this. He saw no point. It was easier just to give up. He withdrew into himself.

"You have to try. I have worked with many whose injuries have been far worse, soldiers with no legs, no arms, men paralysed completely from the neck down. Life will improve, trust me," the physiotherapist said.

Tim was not of a mind to listen He was in that place of self pity that inhibited a vision of a future life. He was in the here and now. He could see no further than a wheelchair and dependency on others for every little thing.

He lay in his bed, looking out through the glass partition to the corridor where Harriet and the doctor were engaged in conversation. He wished they would just leave him alone.

"The most concerning aspect is clearly his mental attitude. The actual damage is not so severe and the brain is remarkable in its ability to generate new neurological pathways to overcome damage. It needs the chance to learn and compensate. That requires physiotherapy. It requires will and determination," said the Consultant.

"In other words he has given up," said Harriet.

"In short yes, he is unwilling to engage in the process."

"What about the psychiatrists, can they do nothing?"

"It is just not that simple. They try but there is a limit. The condition could be solely emotional but there is damage to the brain and that has to be considered. The brain is complex and everyone is different."

"What are you saying?"

"Time is not Mr Burr's friend. The longer he remains inactive the less likely it becomes that his condition will improve."

Harriet looked through the glass at Tim. He was lying on the bed staring into the middle distance locked in a world of his own negative thoughts. He had given up. The spark she knew that had driven him, invigorated him, made him who he was, had been extinguished. She turned her head away and looked at the blank grey wall of the corridor and began to weep.

She took a deep breath, "I won't have it!" She said out loud. "I won't fucking have it. You may have given up but I haven't." She loved this man and she was not letting him go from her life that easily. She pushed the door open and entered the room where he lay.

Through her force of will and perseverance he had made progress. In the end he had come to believe that there was life to be had. Gradually Tim Returned, the Tim Burr that was Director General of MI5, determined, resourceful and intelligence and with a rare sense of irony and wit. Harriet provided the optimism that he lacked and he put in the determination and the hard work began on the road to his recovery.

He was home and he was independent. He got up and with the aid of his walking frame, made the bathroom and completed his morning ablution. He was sat reading the morning papers when the door bell rang.

"Morning," he said as Madeleine Wilson and Harriet Shaw made their way to the dining area where he had placed cups and coffee in anticipation.

Madeleine had taken over as his temporary replacement at MI5. MI5 now had the first black head in its history. She sat and sipped the coffee. "Where do you buy this coffee? It tastes like piss."

"It's not that bad," said Harriet.

"You are just sucking up to him. It's awful."

Tim was officially on sick leave. They would assess his capacity to resume his post over the next few months. In the mean time he met with the acting head once or twice a week to consult. Harriet attended as head of the Cyber-tech division. Strictly speaking there was little need for her to be there and other heads of section would have been more relevant but Madeleine knew there was a bond and Harriet's devotion was helping Tim's recovery.

Tim seemed oblivious to Harriet's love for him. There had been a moment between them previously but it had not developed. In truth he was not allowing himself to grow any feelings towards her. He felt himself damaged, crippled and she was younger and deserved more.

"So apart from holding an unsuccessful coffee morning is there anything I could be of any use in?" asked Tim. He took a mouthful of coffee as he finished the sentence. It was disgusting. "This coffee's perfect. I have no idea what you are on about."

"Right," said Madeleine and took a memory stick from her hand bag. She inserted it into the laptop on the dining table around which they were gathered. The information could have been accessed on line with a link to Madeleine's computer at Thames House, the HQ of MI5 but she preferred to do it this way. The excuse was that a secure link to Tim's home was hard to ensure but the truth was that it gave a social dimension to Tim's life. Face-to-face human interaction was essential to human beings and in his case was therapeutic.

"It's your area." said Harriet. Tim had focussed on the Arab region and had, in his own way, become a bit of an expert in Middle Eastern politics and the interacting forces in play.

Mo's face appeared on the screen along with his activities over the past few days. Tim clicked on file after file containing all that was known on the people who had been monitored. Profile after profile appeared as he clicked through. It was a vast web.

"Well what do you make of it?" said Madeleine.

"Something's definitely up," said Tim

"Well that insight was definitely worth coming here for" laughed Harriet. "We can see why you had the top job at MI5"

Chapter 4

Bangkok airport was hot and crowded. The baggage was backed up and there was hardly room to move in the hall. Matters were worse at customs and immigration. The airport was surrounded by protestors who added to the chaos in and around the airport.

Suzy Webb was tired from the flight of nearly twenty six hours and just wanted to get to the hotel. She was due to meet with two colleagues who had been in Thailand for over a month and had done the preliminary ground work with various Thai Government agencies and private corporations.

She had hoped that there would be someone to meet her as she came in to the Arrivals Hall, a driver with a placard with her name or perhaps a colleague to help her with her luggage and the various cases containing the paperwork. The protests had put a stop to that notion. The arrivals area was sealed off to prevent the protesters organising a sit-in and causing further disruption.

She had no choice but to pull the cart alone. It was a struggle to keep her luggage and the various document cases balanced as she made her way to the airport exit. She finally made it outside. The scene was that of chaos. The roads were blocked in all directions by protestors. She stood on the pavement outside the airport and looked around for her driver. A line of police were advancing across the road and pushing the protestors ahead of them in an attempt to clear the road.

Suzy realised the likelihood was that she would be stuck here for some while. She pulled her largest suitcase from the trolley and, setting it on its end, used it as a makeshift seat. She had tried time and time again to give up smoking but had failed. She lit a cigarette and took a puff. She experienced a satisfying head rush after her prolonged absence owing to the length of the flight.

She had left SO15 over thirteen years ago. Now in her forties she had rebuilt her life after the enquiry into the death of the woman at the Mosque. She had become interested in conservation and the environment. Her interest had led to serious study and then a career. She was now a senior executive with AGENDA, the Asian Green Energy and Development Agency

She had responsibility for the Agency's activities in Thailand. The country was experiencing rapid development as it concentrated on economic growth. It was dependent mostly on fossil fuels, coal and gas, as its energy source. This coupled with its high rate of energy use, almost twice that of the European countries and three times that of Latin American countries, led to considerable greenhouse gas emissions.

Thailand gave its undertaking to reduce its energy intensity by thirty percent by 2036 by the development of solar, wind, biomass energy and waste processing. AGENDA role was to lend its support to reducing energy used in business, commercial and industrial undertakings and private buildings. It offered support, guidance and expertise along with financial incentives and funding. Suzy was in Thailand to arrange credit lines with a number of banks and meet with major industrialist and business leaders to promote the Agency's goals.

She had not got very far. Two hours, some four cups of espresso and half a packet of cigarettes later she was still waiting outside the airport. Then all of a sudden the protestors left. She did not know it but there had been talks, a compromise and a lull in the protests as part of the agreement.

"Ms Webb," said the man in the chauffeur's uniform.

When she finally arrived at her hotel there was given a message at the front desk as she checked in. It said a car would be sent the following morning to take her to her office. The protests had completely disrupted the plans for her arrival and her schedule had been pushed back. She was relieved to have the time to get her bearings before launching into a round of meetings.

She took a bath in her room before unpacking. She had been in the same clothes for nearly two days and it felt good to wash and change. She had no sooner put her blouse and skirt on when the room phone rang.

"Suzy Webb," she answered.

"Miss Webb my name is Somchai Onruang. I was given your hotel number by your office. I represent the Dawar Corporation here in Thailand." he paused, waiting for a response.

The name sounded familiar but she could not bring the details to the fore in her mind. She was unsure how to respond. "Yes Mr Onruang, how may I be of assistance?"

"As I said, I spoke to your office and they suggested I speak with you directly."

"Concerning what exactly?"

"The Dawar Corporation is one of the biggest conglomerates in the country and has seen spectacular growth in the last few years. Apart from the Government, we are the third largest consumer of electricity, if one combines all our operations." He paused and waited for a reaction.

She joined the dots. The Dawar Group was one of the most powerful opponents of the green initiative. It saw it as a costly exercise that it would unfairly be burdened with. It held economic and political sway in the country and was impeding or halting a number of AGENDA's programmes. So far it had adopted an almost hostile approach to its attempts to introduce initiatives for change. Dawar was the key player Suzy knew had to be brought on side if real progress with the Paris Accord was to be made in Thailand.

AGENDA had made numerous approaches to Dawar with no success. Their approaches had, up until now, been met with a stone wall. Suzy realised that with this phone call there was a chance of establishing a channel of communication.

"I understand that you itinerary is restricted to meetings in Bangkok only?"

"I believe so. I am only here for a short period. I am addressing a symposium outlining our function, meeting with Government officials and finalising a large line of credit with the banks to provide funding."

"That is unfortunate. I was hopping that you could find time to visit with us at our base of operations?"

"I am sure my office could find a few hours for us to meet." She did not want to miss any opportunity to enter into dialogue with the Dawar Corporation.

"I was hoping that you would visit our headquarters in Chiang Mai?"

Suzy knew of the province. Despite being a predominantly agricultural region, its levels of air pollution ranked as one of the worst in the Country. The local farmers were not the problem but agricultural corporations such as Dawar were. Year upon year the forest was being burnt to grow, not crops for local consumption such as rice but to grow corn. The Government ignored the issue due to a mix of corruption and lack of resources. It was a key target area for the Agency. She realised the importance of establishing a dialogue and Dawar could hold the key.

"My schedule is tight. As you know, we operate in a number of Asian countries not only Thailand and we have organised a series of events coordinated with other environmental agencies and Ngo's throughout this month in an attempt to push matters foreword. The effective suspension of the United States' participation in the Paris Accord has resulted in a more intensive approach by the other participants." She knew the importance of reluctance in dealing with large corporation as a negotiating tool. Be too keen and they push for more money and less commitment.

"I understand. I feel that there is progress to be made in face-to-face discussions."

"I don't understand why we cannot meet here in Bangkok?"

"I think I failed to make myself clear. It is not I with whom you are to meet. Mr Dawar is to be in Chiang Mai and is attending Yi Peng. It is a local festival and Dawar Corporation is sponsoring a gathering of its business partners from around the globe. He intends to afford you the opportunity to address delegates from China, India, and Pakistan and across Asia. It is a golden opportunity to meet and promote your aims at the highest corporate level. These, Ms Webb, are the people that wield power and pull at the strings of government in their various countries."

"I knew nothing of this meeting."

"Why should you. It primary aim is to promulgate business between its participants, not save the planet. I believe this a real opportunity for you to go straight to the horses mouth. I think that is the saying."

"They also say you can lead a horse to water but you cannot make it drink."

Chapter 5

He had seen nothing like it before. It was a world that only existed in films. Ibrahim Dawar knew he was out of his league as he walked through the lobby of the Four Season Hotel in Macau. It was a Friday night and the businessmen from Hong Kong were streaming into the Cotai Strip, Macau for the weekend. He had flown from Bangkok and had been met at the airport and driven to the hotel. His overnight bag had been whisked to his suite and with no delay he had been escorted to his room.

He had, of course, seen films based in Las Vegas but he had not expected to find it reproduced here on China's doorstep. He was not poor by Pakistani standards or by many other standards for that matter but the feeling of wealth here was all encompassing. He sat and stared out over the sky scrapers through the vast window. Ibrahim felt the tension in his stomach. Things were moving fast and he was getting in deeper.

In the normality of things he would never have contemplated the course of action that he was set on. But normality had been destroyed for him a number of years earlier. His life had changed and everything he held dear had been snatched from him. That day he had taken an oath before God that he would get justice but justice costs money. Now, so many years later he had the chance of getting enough.

He had built a small mining business in Pakistan. The family land had been unpromising but his father had found nephrite or jade. There are two types of jade, nephrite and jadeite, the more valuable and dearer than gold is jadeite. Ibrahim's quarry would never make him rich but it did allow him to grow his business.

The Dawar Corporation's business was no longer focussed on the mining but had expanded into Thailand and its HQ was in Chiang Mai. On paper, the company was one of the largest in its sector. Accounts can be misleading. The company was broke. Clever accounting and special purpose companies scattered around Countries with little or no reporting requirements allowed the Dawar Corporation to hide the true state of its financial losses. Bribery and corruption took care of the rest.

Ibrahim was here in Macau as a last desperate roll of the dice. The irony was that he did not care a jot for the money, the Company or life itself for that matter. His only purpose for living was to make good his promise to God over ten years ago.

He started as the phone rang. "Show them up," he told the voice at the end of the phone.

After what seemed an hour but was less than a few minutes there was a knock. He took a deep breath and looked in a mirror. He ran his hand through his hair and checked his beard for crumbs or any other inhabitants. He made himself smile. It definitely would not do to open the door with remains of his sandwich trapped in the hair or his chin. He remembered his mother berating him as a child about the slovenliness of his eating habits. The thought of her steadied his nerves as he let his guests in.

The doorway was filled with the tallest, widest and most powerfully built individual he had ever encountered. He stepped into the room and walked straight past him. He was followed by as second such individual who just filled the doorway and stood stock still. The first inspected every inch of the suite while the second taciturnly patted down Ibrahim in a search for presumably weapons or perhaps a wire tap?

With a nod from the first the second cleared the entrance; A third smaller Chinese man with tiny spectacles entered the room. He walked confidently into the centre of the room. "My name is General Xi." He extended his hand. He like Ibrahim spoke English and this was to be their chosen language of communication.

Ibrahim was slightly wrong footed. This unassuming small man was far from what he had envisaged. His stature belayed the power he wielded. He shared not only a name with the Chinese Premier but also his ear. He was the fixer for the rich and powerful.

"I hope you find the accommodation adequate?" He looked around the suite as though he had entered a hovel rather than a five star room. He gave the impression that he would never lower himself to stay in such a meagre abode.

"It is fine." Ibrahim tried to convey an air that this was the norm for him and that he was accustomed to wealth.

Xi just smiled. He has Chinese Intelligence at his beck and call and knew that the man before him was virtually bankrupt. "I am glad."

There was an awkward silence. Ibrahim felt uncomfortable as the small man just sat and stared at him, sizing him up. He had to fill the gap. "Can I get you something, a drink perhaps?"

"You drink? I did not think your sort drank."

In that instant he knew that the man before had no respect for him whatsoever. Xi considered anything but Chinese as inferior and Muslims towards the bottom of the list. There could be no trust here. There was only business. Given the choice he would have nothing to do with this General but he had no other way out.

The General continued either not aware of or indifferent to the offence he had caused. Ibrahim suspected the latter. "To business, as you know we have panache for quality items in China. Traditionally jade is a special part of our heritage. We highly prize it both aesthetically and spiritually."

"But the stone you want is jadeite. My poor mines in Pakistan cannot meet your requirements."

"There are certain complications with the current supply chain. We are exploring alternatives."

"I am unclear as to you concerns."

"Myanmar or Burma has always been a source of the jadeite so dear to us. We particularly like the green. Ninety per cent of the export of Jade from Burma is smuggled to China and never appears in the official Government figures. We had our own deals with the military there."

"So what had changed?"

"Nothing has changed. It is a very cosy set up. Let us just say it makes some people very rich and others not so."

"And you fall into the latter category?" said Ibrahim. Xi shifted uncomfortably in his seat. Ibrahim realised he should be more careful in his choice of words. The Chinese did not like to lose face and Xi in particular was a very proud man.

"Not exactly how I would put it. We are interested in opening alternative routes for the importation of Jade that do not involve the existing Myanmar and Chinese military cartel. We feel that you are the person to help."

"How can I help?" Ibrahim noted the first sign of weakness in the man before him, a level of tension. Xi depended on his wealth and his health by fulfilling the needs and desires of the elite that ran China. If he couldn't deliver he would be replaced and some trumped up corruption charge used to get him out of the way with minimum fuss and bother. He was totally dependent on the good will of others to keep his wealth.

"You can help by bringing us the Jade from Burma."

Chapter 6

Madeleine Wilson took the Chair as acting Deputy General of MI5. It was the regular monthly meeting of the Management Board. It was not an unfamiliar role for her. Even when Tim had been running the show, unless there was a real crisis, he would send her in his stead. A great deal of the meeting's time would always be devoted to finance. There was never enough money, staff or resources and always too many demands to be met.

Every meeting was attended by the Agency's legal advisors. There were many occasions when a course of action would be considered and could not be pursued after legal consideration. MI5 was within the remit of the Home Secretary and was ultimately accountable to the electorate. Its actions needed to stay within the law. Life of course would be far easier if it could do want it wanted or needed to do.

MI5 had far reaching powers but it worked within the framework of a parliamentary democracy. Exceeding the limits of legality would be a home goal. If it undermined its own legitimacy it would be no better than the people and foreign agencies from which it looked to protect the Country and its citizens. It would be doing their work for them.

Tim, in a less than conventional move had appointed Harriet Shaw to act as his deputy in situ. Madeleine was acting head and her role as Deputy Director General was vacant. It remained vacant and this was as a stop gap while his future capacity was determined. Harriet, in effect, was acting as a liaison between Tim and the Board.

Harriet's role as head of Cyber Counter-Espionage and Counter Proliferation had meant there had been the need for a shuffle around in that department in order to free her up. Tim called her his carer.

The meeting came to order and the Management Board now consisted of Madeleine as Acting Deputy General, the senior lawyer, with a flock of minions sat behind him to check the final points of the law, the Director General Capability and the Director General Strategy and Tim's carer in Chief, Harriet.

The purpose of the meetings held monthly was to consider policy and strategic issues and adapt them to various threats. In fact, as usual the first hour was taken up by cuts, costs and overruns and legal issues. In truth, like most Government Agencies, it could be summed up in a very short sentence: too much work, not enough money to do it.

Eventually the members managed get around to dealing with the actual threats.

"Arnold, tell us what you make of it" said Madeleine.

The Deputy General Strategy began to speak. "We have a very confused picture. Within a matter of days it would appear that a couple of basically low risk students in Luton have triggered an alert for a massive terrorist plot, involving ten, twenty, who knows at this stage, cells Nationwide. It grows daily."

The DG Capability interrupted, "there must have previous Intel, surely?"

"Tom" Arnold responded directly to his counterpart. "It took us completely by surprise. I assure you."

"I just cannot believe that none of this was picked up, what about GCHQ Cheltenham? Surely they must have picked up on some chatter electronically."

"Not a sausage, they are on it now but it seems to have not to have gone down the normal communication pattern of communication, which their algorithms are structured to identify. There was limited traffic between our potential terrorists and the usual ISIS radical dark web communication channels. This threat has materialised, as it were, rapidly and is fully formed and organised." said Arnold.

Tom spoke "It has to be funded somehow?"

"Clearly and we have everyone trying to trace the money. It is a conundrum. The almost total defeat of the Islamic State fighters in Iraq and Syria and the taking back of the oil fields have cut off their supply of funds. Recently terrorist attacks have been low tech carried out by individuals identifying with ISIS philosophy but not really connected organisationally or financially."

"This goes against the norm then," said Madeleine. "Well coordinated and well financed. Someone is providing millions to do this. It has to be State sponsored."

"Who, the Saudis, the Iraqis?"

"Not at this juncture," said Tom. "It is not in either of their interests."

Madeleine sat in her office with Harriet. The meeting had closed with no real advance or plausible theory as to the new threat. The clear message that did emerge was that MI5 resources were stretched to the limit and they were struggling to keep pace with events.

"What will you say to Tim when you see him later?" Madeleine asked.

"What is there to be said, that we are up shit creek without a paddle?"

"We have to be missing something. This had been a long time in planning. You can't recruit twenty, thirty or forty people in five minutes. It takes time, a lot of time."

"The numbers seemingly involved would surely have resulted in a leak. This would have been picked by us or the police. Nothing can be kept this quiet. It is just not possible," said Harriet.

"But it must be possible because three days ago we knew nothing and today we have to devote most of our resources tracking it."

"We need Tim's mind on this" said Harriet.

"Our secret weapon, Mr Devious mind in Chief," laughed Madeleine.

"He says it's the little details that get you there."

"Now he's bloody Sherlock Homes?"

"Hardly, it's that he has a different background to the rest of you. He thinks laterally."

"As I said he is devious."

"Shall I tell him that?"

"Best not," said Madeleine, "but you are right we do need his insight on this. Get over to his house and get him linked up to the data and reports here."

"Right, you do realise that I shall probably have to print it all off and put it in buff folders for him. He hates reading from a screen."

After Harriet left she remained deep in thought for a few minutes. She realised that she could not take the role of Director General permanently. She would love to have the job but she knew that it was a step too far. The administration was already beginning to overwhelm her. She understood that you needed not only a certain level of intellect to do the job but also key personality traits that allowed you to step back and grasp the overall picture.

The job was as much about politics as it was spy craft. The incumbent had to balance the political demands and perceptions of the Government of the day with the true demands of keeping the Country and its citizens safe. The two were often at variance and treading the line was stressful. Tim seemed to let it all go over his head and naturally keep all the plates spinning almost effortlessly.

She took a deep breath and a sip of coffee and decided to take her mind off things for a bit by reading the latest news headlines. Strictly Come Dancing the celebrity dance competition was back on the television. The news was full of the latest gossip from the programme. One of the dancers and one of the celebrities had been caught doing more than a tango. It took her mind off the pressing temporarily as she

Jade

read the details.

Chapter 7

2007

"Can't you go any faster? We will be missing the plane at this rate," said Mina.

The taxi driver raised his hands. "I can only go as fast as the traffic allows." The traffic at that moment was allowing no progress what so ever. A lorry had shed part of its load onto the carriageway. The lorry driver was engaged in a fierce shouting match with the driver of the tuk-tuk, which had pulled across him and caused him to swerve. The roads in Pakistan played host to every conceivable mode of transport from mopeds to horse and cart. The most popular way of getting about was provided by the tuk-tuk, a hybrid of a scooter and a tricycle with a cab roof over it.

"We have plenty of time" said Sami. She was accompanying her sister and her sister's daughter Javeria to England. Her son Reza, the groom awaited his cousin in London. They had never met but it was a good match.

"It is such a pity that Papa could not come" said Javeria.

"You know we cannot afford it. He has to work. Weddings are not cheap," said her Mother.

"What is London like, Auntie?"

Sami thought for a while before replying. "There is work but the weather is terrible, cold and wet," she smiled.

"Well I am glad I asked," said Javeria with a hint of sarcasm.

The traffic began to move and soon the signs for the airport appeared alongside the road. "Not so far now," said the driver.

Mina, Javeria's mother had also never been to England. In fact she had hardly left the village where she had been born. Her marriage had been arranged and she was pregnant by the time she was fifteen. It had been a difficult birth and consequently Javeria was their only child. Her husband was a good man. Despite the fact she could never give him a son. He had not divorced and remarried. Javeria was the centre of his life and he was devoted to his daughter.

He wanted a better life for his daughter. They were not poor but life was still harsh and difficult. They had saved and worked and hoped for a good match for their daughter. Reza was suggested and accepted by the families.

While Mina had been the obedient daughter her sister Sami was the more adventurous. She had found her own husband. She had persuaded her father to let her travel to England and marry Reza's father, a restaurateur in London's East End. When her son needed a bride she had immediately thought of her niece.

She was proud of her son. He had done well at school and had a job in PR in the West End. He was still a good Muslim, attending the Mosque regularly and not drinking despite the temptations on offer in the City. Now he would have a decent Muslim wife from a good family.

She had arranged for Javeria to stay with a distant relative of her husbands while the couple got to know each other, chaperoned of course. Her sister, Mina would stay there too. The wedding was set for just over a month's time. If her brother-in-law could raise the money, he would fly over for the ceremony but that seemed less than likely.

There was a queue of taxis and cars waiting to get to the drop-off point outside the airport. Javeria looked from the rear window of the taxi. She took in her last view of the Country she had been raised in. She felt apprehensive. She knew her parents knew best but it still felt strange, boarding a plane and leaving her homeland.

Her parents had ensured she had an education. With no brothers, she had been fortunate in that way. Many girls her age would already be married with children. She was coming up to nineteen and had gone to a good school. Her father, either by good judgement or luck, had made sure she had studied English. Her mother, by contrast, could not read or write in any language. Her aunt Sámi had learnt English and attended classes In England that had taught her to write. Her future husband suffered from none of these difficulties. English was his first language. He had been to university after school and England was his home.

They finally unloaded their luggage from the taxi. Mina and Javeria were at a loss as what to do next. Sami took the lead and led them towards the departure lounge. They tagged along behind like children on a day out at some attraction. They had not a clue what they were doing and just followed her.

Visas had been difficult. Mina had a visitors and Javier had a student visa. There were difficulties in travelling to Britain to marry. Immigration was a hot political topic and rules were tight. Her future husband was a British national as were his parents. They would marry and the lawyers employed by her father-in-law to be, were optimistic in getting her at least permanent leave to remain in the country.

Clearing security took over an hour and they felt like they had been travelling for days by the time they actually reached the Departure Lounge. Their journey stretched ahead for many hours. They had a stop over in Istanbul for nearly five hours before their onward flight to Heathrow, the airport on the outskirts of London.

The excitement of flying soon evaporated with the cramped conditions on the planes, the delays and the poor food. By the time they were in the terminal at Heathrow they felt as though they had been dragged through a car wash and then hung out to dry in a dusty building site. Mina and Javeria again followed Sami as she led them to the Piccadilly line underground. The excitement of the tube soon wore off as it trundled its way into central London. Eventually over twenty six hours after they had set out they arrived in the East End completely exhausted.

The following weeks seem to flash by. "Do we know these people?" Javeria asked Reza as they sat in his father's restaurant at one of the tables.

He was holding the guest list for the wedding and sitting by a pile of invites waiting to be signed and despatched. "Not a clue, Mum says they are cousins, aunts and uncles."

"Right, it seems a list of every Pakistani in the Country," she laughed.

"Probably is, their definition of cousin extends to ninety three removed. A wedding is a big social event. It reminds and connects their generation with their home and culture."

"I know. It is all so different and strange here," she said.

"But you like it?"

"I like you."

"I love you," he replied. If there was such a thing as love at first sight Javeria and Reza seemed to have fallen for it. Impartially the concept of familiar attraction may have played its part but what ever the reason the attraction was deep and instant.

They were both sure and just wanted to be together. For their parents, it was a perfect match and the wedding preparation went into full swing

"Mum thanks you again for the phone. She can't stop playing with it. She thinks it is magic the way it takes photos. She is like a woman possessed. Did you know it can take videos as well?" said Javeria.

"Of course it is the latest Nokia N95 it's amazing and just the thing to get into your future mother-in-law's good books," he laughed. "And my Mum says she is organising a party so you can get to know the locals."

"Cousins I suspect."

"It's in a meeting room above the Mosque. You could make it a party even if it's not officially an engagement party. Have fun and meet the wives and daughters of the congregation... It could be fun."

It did not sound that much fun to Javeria. More like she was to be paraded to satisfy local curiosity but she would throw herself into it anyway. "Okay I'll make food and get some balloons."

"Just get the balloons. I'll get Dad to sort the food from the restaurant." She looked dubious.

"It will be proper home food not the stuff he serves in the restaurant."

The day of the engagement party came. The room was packed and the chatter incessant. Javeria had been right in her assessment. She was being paraded by aunt Sami as some prize catch for her son. She could not remember all the names of the women or their relationship to her and each other. She had to admit that it did have a flavour of home about it. The sort of gatherings they had in the village. London can be a very lonely place even if you are surrounded by millions of people daily. Many of the women rarely moved outside their own circle and spoke little or no English. Their husbands did not encourage it.

"Silence silence!" Sami called. "Everybody, this is Javeria and she is to be my son's wife."

The door flew open as the party poppers were pulled. There was a burst of gunfire, stunned silence, followed by screaming.

A young girl lay dead. A father had lost a daughter and a young man a future wife.

Chapter 8

"Well how did it go," said Somchai Onruang as Ibrahim Dawar sat down at his desk, in his office in the Company's HQ building in Chiang Mai. He was tired from the flight back from Hong Kong and his meeting with the Chinese.

He paused before he spoke. He lent back in his chair. He was not sure how the meeting had gone. He had gone to Macau knowing what to expect. Dawar Corporation was broke and he needed the money. What he did not need was the spotlight shined on him and his business affairs. The accounts were pure fiction and would not stand up to a moment's scrutiny. He had spent over ten years of his life building to this point in time.

He had built the Company from scratch. In the beginning, he had dug the rocks himself in the hills in Pakistan, selling lumps of jade to local buyers. Gradually over the years his business had grown. He had moved the operation to Thailand using every last penny and mortgaging to the hilt. The company's operation in Chiang Mai was a failure. He had gambled everything and lost. His time was running out and he had a promise to fulfil. He needed money and he would do what it took to get it.

It was a one shot deal and it all hinged on Xi and his cronies in China. The Chinese had been working jade for over 5000 years. The jade they wanted came from Myanmar and they could get it. The price had rocketed to over $3,000 an ounce, hundreds of times the price of gold. Dewar's mines in Pakistan produced nephrite worth a fraction of the price of Myanmar Jadeite.

"They want the jade. We have to get it to them," said Ibrahim.

Somchai Onruang sat silent as he digested the statement. The rewards would be massive and he knew that he would be a rich man but the risks were massive as well, "that is a big ask."

"It was not a negotiation. There was one option on the table. They want the Jade out of Burma and delivered to them - over ten tons of it."

Somchai went pale. "Ten fucking tons of top quality Jade. That's not possible."

"Well it seems that it is and they did not seem to be the type of people with a sense of humour."

Somchai digested what he had been told. He started to speak and stopped himself. He started to speak again and hesitated. He finally found his voice. "And you said we could get it for them?"

"I did. We just have to go and get it, bring it over the Thai border and ship it to China"

"You do realise that if we are caught that will be over a billion dollars of illegal jade we will have in our possession? People die very easily for that sort of money," said Somchai.

Ibrahim said nothing and turned his palms face up and shrugged. There was a small part of his discussion with the Chinese he had not bothered to mention to Somchai. It would not have pleased him but ignorance is bliss. There was something Ibrahim wanted more than money and the General was in a position to make it happen. He had made a deal, a trade. General Xi had access to something he wanted and they had come to arrangement.

They sat in silence for a while. Then Somchai spoke, "okay how is it to be done?"

"The long way round obviously, they can't get it across the Chinese border or they wouldn't need us. We bring it into Thailand and ship it to China."

"So how do we ship ten ton of illegal rock that we don't have in the first place?"

"But we do," said Ibrahim. "We are currently awaiting the arrival of a shipment of nephrite from our mines in Pakistan, all above board."

"You are transiting through Thailand. How does that get us any further?" said Somchai.

"It wouldn't apart from the deal I have struck with a port official. The cargo is in bond but we will be allowed to swap the box so to speak." A smile spread across Ibrahim's face.

"The manifest ties up, the Chinese get their priceless Jadeite and the nephrite ends up at the bottom of the sea."

"And we end up fifty million dollars to the good." Ibrahim lied. He had traded the money for General Xi's alternative payment.

"Makes what I have to tell you seem insignificant now," said Somchai.

"What that?"

"Well I was trying to think of ways to somehow get some money in from somewhere. I made contact with the Asian Green Energy Development Agency and made you an appointment."

Ibrahim looked blank. "And what, they are just going to give Dawar money?"

"In essence yes, Thailand is part of the Paris agreement on Climate Change, he pulled a piece of paper from his pocket and read, "Thailand has undertaken to diversify its sources of energy and to develop solar and wind power, as well as power from biomass and waste processing. It is aiming for a 30% reduction in energy intensity by 2036."

"Sounds impressive," said Ibrahim.

"AGENDA has established credit lines with a bank in Thailand and the money is just sitting there for us to use. The deal you have done with your Chinese mates makes this look like peanuts now though."

 "So what have you done?"

"We have an appointment with a Suzy Webb later. She is at the hotel or should be by now. She had to travel up alone so I said we would have a preliminary meeting and show her a bit of Chiang Mai before getting down to some real work tomorrow.," said Somchai.

"Who exactly is she?"

"She is heading up the initiative for AGENDA in Asia and specifically Thailand. I got in first so we could be first in line for a big payout for cleaning up operations and getting the corporation into this biomass stuff, millions."

Ibrahim was in no mood to be entertaining. He was tired from his flight and stressed. "Do I have to?" he asked.

"It won't be that bad. Don't forget it is Yi Peng after all."

"What's that?" said Ibrahim.

Somchai explained that Ty Peng was a festival held on the full moon and the Thais float banana-leaf containers with flowers and candles in the rivers to worship the Goddess of Water. Lanna-style lanterns, hot-air balloons made of paper, were launched into the air.

 "Okay we could do with a blessing from a Goddess," said Ibrahim.

"Not forgetting the money on offer from AGENDA."

Chapter 9

"Do these buggers never go out?"

"Doesn't look like it. They aren't even going to prayers."

"Unbelievable, call themselves Jihadis and they don't even go to the Mosque. They are a bloody disgrace to any self respecting terrorist."

The two MI5 surveillance experts had been parked outside the terraced house in Luton for nearly three days. Their vehicle was an old white transit van and with the dents and rust it blended perfectly with the other vehicles that were parked in the streets in the area. Since Mo's visit to the address, the location and its occupants had been watched round the clock and followed wherever they went. They never left the flat unguarded. One of the tenants remained in the house at all times.

The phone and electronic taps were yielding little information. They were well instructed in the dangers of the ability of the secret service's ability to track and monitor their computers, tablets and phones and kept their communications clean. The same was true at the other locations Mo had subsequently visited.

The Police and MI5 had the same problem at the other identified locations as a result of following Mo. Warrants had been granted allowing microphones and cameras to be installed inside each of the suspect's homes but gaining access without arousing suspicion was proving almost impossible.

The threat they posed was as yet unquantifiable. MI5 had no target identified, no time frame and no inkling as to the type of threat. They did not have sufficient evidence to arrest the suspects or raid their homes. They were unsure if they had identified all those involved. Before any action could be taken they needed total certainty they had everyone. If any of the potential terrorists were not rounded up in a single swoop then the threat would still be active and worse, MI5 would have no idea who was still out there posing a risk.

"Looks like another wasted day. We just have to hand over to the night shift soon and hope they have better luck" said the agent.

A young woman with black hair and a man a few years older were making their way up the street. The man was using a walking cane to aid his progress. Their progress was slow and the man seemed to be having difficulty in walking. The watchers observed them as they reached the small wall that bordered the property where the suspects lived.

The row of terraced houses all originally had the same small walls when they were built at the turn of the twentieth century. Each had its own small garden to the front when they were constructed, now most had their walls removed and the garden concreted over to provide for parking or an area for dustbins. Most of the houses had been converted into apartments and were let to students. The suspect house, along with just a few others, still had its wall in tact.

The man suddenly seemed to have difficulties and began to shake. His companion helped him to sit on the wall. Matters seemed to be escalating as the man's condition worsened. The woman was clearly beginning to panic and was attempting to loosen his clothing. He seemed to lose all control of his body and fell backwards over the wall onto the garden.

"Help!" the woman began to scream frantically.

"What do we do now?" the watcher in the van said.

His colleague was hesitant, unsure how to respond. If they suddenly appeared from a builder's van carrying a defibrillator and medical kit their cover would be blown. It was a stark choice, stand by and watch someone die or blow the entire operation. "We sit it out. There are too many potential lives at risk."

"Jesus Christ!" said his companion. They sat helpless and watched the scene play out on the street before them

The woman was frantic, screaming and trying to get her companion into the recovery position. He was too heavy or she was too weak. In any event, she could not do it and the man lay, fitting in the yard.

The door eventually opened and the one suspect who had remained in the property appeared in the doorway. "Help me!" the young woman screamed at the Asian man in the doorway. "He is having a heart attack."

He stood in the doorway, hesitating. People were beginning to look from their windows and doors were opening in response to her screaming. He wanted to close the door and go inside. He wanted no part of the drama that was unfolding. He couldn't. To just close the door on a man dying in your garden would have drawn even more attention and raised suspicion. Reluctantly, he came to the screaming woman's aid.

"Help me get him inside out of the cold," she said. She began to lift his feet. He had no choice. He put his arms under his shoulders and together they carried him into the flat.

"Call an ambulance," she instructed as she began CPR. "Now!" she shouted. She had taken total control of the situation and he obeyed. He dialled 999 and gave his location.

"Ten minutes," he said. She nodded.

The voice at the end of the phone began instructing him as to what he should do while waiting for the paramedics to arrive. "Take over" she instructed as she put the phone on loud speaker.

The instructions came thick and fast down the phone from the medic on the other end. "Check his airway, loosen his clothing, is he breathing?" He was sweating with the stress of the situation and trying to follow the instructions precisely.

The woman returned with pillows and blankets from one of the bedrooms. She threw them down, disappeared and later returned with water which she spilt. He realised that she was hysterical and doing things randomly in a vain attempt to help. "Stop it" he said. "You are distracting me. I can't hear what is being said on the phone."

She looked frantic but finally focussed on what he had said. She disappeared, presumably outside to await the arrival of the ambulance. He refocused on the telephone and the instructions coming from the operator. The man's condition seemed to be worsening despite his efforts.

The irony was not lost him. Here he was doing all he could to save the life of one enemy that in a day or a week he would be killing on mass.

Finally the ambulance crew arrived and he stepped aside to allow them room to work. They worked in a coordinated scripted choreography. He watched as the man was stabilised, drips inserted and a stretcher was brought. He held the door and he watched as the man, the paramedics and the woman disappeared into the ambulance. There was the sound of the ambulance warning bells and the flashing light. Then all was silent. He went back inside and closed the door.

"Bloody hell," said the watcher in the van.

"That was different. What are the odds of that happening?" came the reply.

Before he could answer their conversation was interrupted by control. They looked at one another with questioning confusion. "Just do it, please, now," came the slightly irritated voice when he asked for confirmation.

They drove three streets away and parked. "That's it," said the agent in the passenger seat. The driver watched as the passenger got out and approached a parked jaguar XF. He tried the door and it opened. The electronic key fob had been left in the glove compartment.

He sat in the driver's seat and pressed the start button. The engine started. He gave the thumbs up to the agent in the van, who drove off.

He drove to the Queen Elizabeth II hospital and pulled up outside the Accident and Emergency Department. The white van had already arrived driven there by his fellow agent. He jumped at the tap on his window.

"Out you pop," said the woman who had been screaming over her dying companion outside the terrorist's house fifteen minutes earlier.

He got out and stood before her. "Fuck me," he said.

"That's no way to speak to your immediate boss and the Director General," said Harriet Shaw and laughed.

Thanks for retrieving our car.," said Tim as he walked past him to the passenger side. "You and your colleague can clock off now. We planted the bugs in the flat for you."

"Sir" said the agent as he made his way back to the white van.

"If you want a job doing well, you might as well do it yourself," said Harriet as she started the engine.

"I should get an Oscar for that performance at the flat," said Tim.

"Only as best supporting actor though, I did all the work planting the bugs" she said as they made their way back to London.

Chapter 10

2007

The press had gathered outside the Coroner's Court on Popular Road in East London. It was a scene that had been repeated for the last six days. It was a national story attracting the attention of both television and the newspapers. Photography and filming are banned in the UK courts so the reporters were restricted to ambushing the participants as the entered and left the building.

Javeria's mother Mina, aunt Sami and her bereaved fiancé Reza fought their way through the swarm of reporters, the microphones being pushed in their faces and the flashing of cameras to the Court steps. The inquest into Javeria's shooting had started speedily. The authorities were determined to conclude the matter as quickly as possible. The mood was unsympathetic as the Country and the World experienced wave after wave of killings carried out by the Islamic extremists.

It was evident from the start to Mina and her family that prejudice would be the overriding sentiment that dominated the proceedings into her daughters shooting. The case had already been tried and judged in the press and public opinion.

Today was a pivotal point in the proceedings. Today was the day when the officer who had fired the fatal shot that killed Mina's daughter would give evidence. It was a day when the lawyer acting for the family of the deceased would have the opportunity to put questions to the person who had actually fired the fatal shot killing the young bride to be at her party. The Coroner's Court was not conducting a trial. It was not in the business of convicting and handing down punishment. Its purpose was to investigate a death and conclude the nature and cause.

Mina, Sami and Reza took their seats. There was not a vacant place to be seen in the packed room. The coroner eventually took the chair and the proceedings commenced.

"There will be a small recess while preparations are made for the next witness. The court will be cleared for the interim." He announced.

No sooner had the proceedings begun and everyone seated than they were adjourned. Everyone, including Javeria's family traipsed from the room and congregated in the lobby. There was the general hubbub of people milling about with no purpose tempered by an overriding sense of anticipation. It had the effect of introducing a sense of theatre into the otherwise dry and stilted process.

The call went out by the Clerk for the displaced to return to the court room. They made their way back to their seats. A screen had been erected in one corner. The witness was to give evidence anonymously. No name and no clue to the identity of the shooter were to be revealed. The officer that fired the fatal shot was to be protected unlike Mina's daughter.

The evidence began. Suzy Webb sat behind the screen. She had her notes in front of her. She had been coached and prepared for the questions. She began to read at the request to recount her version of event the fateful evening Javeria had been shot and killed.

Her statement was long and detailed and covered every aspect   of the raid on the Mosque. Its aim was all to clear. It clearly demonstrated that all those entering the building were aware and fearful of encountering armed and murderous terrorists. It left in no doubt that the officers were facing the real prospect of injury or death. Her statement stressed the accuracy of the underlying intelligence and the in depth risk assessment that had been undertaken prior to the start of operations. All had been briefed that they were at risk and that risk was at its maximum.

By the time she had finished outlining the series of events that led up to Javeria's death, it was time to adjourn for lunch. The room was cleared and again Mina, Sami and Reza found themselves in the lobby.

"She will have to answer questions this afternoon," said Reza.

Sami answered her son while Mina just looked into the middle distance. All she could see was her beautiful daughter's face, her excitement of meeting new friends that day, her joy at her impending wedding then the sight of her broken dead body. "There is no way the truth will not come out. She did nothing. She was killed, murdered without a seconds thought by that bitch behind the screen. It will come out. I believe that," said Sami.

Mina was not so sure. Her own recollection of events was confused. It had all happened so fast. They had been talking and children playing. Then the door had flown open. A dark clad figure, face obscured by a helmet had burst through the door. Screaming and confusion and the sound of a burst of gunfire stopped the revelry.

She had not even seen her daughter shot. She had not realised that anyone was shot. It was all confusion and shouting. They had been driven from the room by the officers, anonymous figures wearing protective armour and helmets. Only as they were herded into custody, had she realised that her daughter was not among them.

It was not until she was released several hours later that she leaned that her daughter was dead, shot and killed. Then it began. The police began looking for evidence to link her and any family members to terrorist activity.

No stone was left unturned. The police were determined to find her daughter's connection to ISIS or Al Qaeda. Her entire life, her family's life and anyone they had contact was put under the microscope. It was clear that they were looking for anything to link them to some form of terrorist activity. Their investigation had revealed nothing.

They sat back in the court room. They had been unable to leave the building for lunch. They felt they could not face the blockade of the press. As Mina sat, tired, grieving and hungry the moment eventually arrived when the facts would be revealed.

"Tell me officer x," their lawyer began his questions. "Tell me the nature of the warning you issued before you fired."

"Armed police, police do not move."

"Are you sure? Numerous witnesses have stated that heard no such warning and only became aware of your presence with the sound of you discharging your weapon?"

"I am perfectly clear. I issued the warning," replied Suzy.

"How do you account for that fact that no one heard the warning?"

There was a moment's pause from behind the screen. "I can only repeat that the correct protocol was followed, any other comment would just be speculation on my part."

"In your statement you say you saw a flash and heard a shot. You then fired at Javeria Kathia."

"Yes," said Suzy.

"Did you see the gun?" asked the lawyer.

"Yes,"

"Again, how do you account for the fact that none of the other people saw a gun or saw or heard any gunfire?"

"I saw the female fire the gun at me so I returned fire in self defence."

The lawyer for the Javeria Kathia family battled on determinedly but in vain. Suzy stuck to her well rehearsed replies and refused to be drawn. It was a blank wall and he finally sat. The matter was adjourned until the next day.

Mina left feeling sick and dashed to the toilet. She just made it to the cubicle. She retched into the bowl. Her head was spinning. She knew there was no gun. It was lies. She knew at some point after they had all been arrested and the room sealed that some one had returned and put a gun in her daughter's hand. She knew that her daughter's murderer would walk away.

Her head was spinning. She felt as though she was being dragged down and down into a spinning pit of despair. She could breathe in the tiny toilet. She needed fresh air. She pushed at the window in the wall to one side. It at first, refused to open. In frustration she threw her shoulder at it. It flew back, almost smashing as it came free.

She needed to hear her husband's voice. She pulled her phone from her bag and took in the deep breaths of the cool clear air as she waited for it to connect with Pakistan. She steadied herself against the open window as she swayed feeling sick at all the lies that she had been forced to listen to in the Court.

There would be no justice for her daughter. She had been killed but no one would be held accountable. The authorities had banded together to cover the matter up. Javeria would be branded a Jihadi, a potential killer and there was nothing she could do about it.

"Well done, you did well," she heard voices approaching.

Looking from the window she could see the black van parked surrounded by armed police. "I don't want to go through that again," a woman's voice replied.

Mina froze, she felt as though she had been punched in the stomach and her breath knocked from her. That voice was the voice she had heard for the last six hours. It was the voice from behind the courtroom screen. It was the voice of her daughter's murderer

She looked at the phone and clicked the call to her husband off. Her daughter's killer was getting closer. The van side door was pulled back to allow her entry. She would be driven away in the blacked out van, her identity remaining a secret for ever.

She realised she had her phone ready. She switched to camera and pressed video. She pointed the phone at the van doors and ducked down from view from the outside. She filmed as Suzy came past and made her way to the van.

Looking up at the camera's screen, she could clearly see her daughter's killer as she left the court and made her way to the van. In a few days her life would be back to normal. She would be free. She would have a life, love, marriage, children and grand children. Javeria had been denied all by this woman. She would only have a funeral pyre and an epitaph calling to the World that she was a terrorist. The van drove off. Mina stopped filming and retched once more into the toilet as tears ran down her face.

Chapter 11

Mo had become aware of his MI5 watchers. They were good but they only had so many people they could assign to him. More to the point they only had a limited number of agents of Indian or Pakistani decent.

Travelling the trains, shopping or just walking in the streets where the population was in the majority white, made it easy for MI5 to remain anonymous. Mosques and clubs where there were no white faces posed the problem.

The Agency had striven to combat the fundamentalist Islamic threat by recruiting more ethnic minorities into their ranks. That takes time, time to recruit and time to train. There were still insufficient trained agents to do the job

Mo was in Southgate in North London. There was not an area with a large Pakistani population. Like London as a whole there was however a wide ethnic mix Turkish, Indian and Afro Caribbean. There was however a one place that was different, the social club.

Not all Muslims are good Muslims and some Muslims like a drink. They try and keep it to themselves. Being seen staggering from the local public house by the Imam was not to be recommended. There were places though where the more liberal could go, away from prying eyes. In Southgate there were two buildings just off the park. One was a clinic specialising in drink and drug rehabilitation the other was a private members club whose membership was predominantly from the Indian continent.

Mo sat at one of the tables eating. The food was Halal the drink that was served was not. Mo was a good Muslim and he knew he needed to be sober. He sat in the far side of the room where the dining tables where. There where sofas and chairs distributed around the room where groups of men sat, talked, smoked and drank.

It was not long before a familiar face appeared. A face Mo had seen time and time again as he visited the various cells around the Country. He was one of the five Asian MI5 operatives who had been tracking him. There was now no doubt now in Mo's mind that he had been rumbled by the Security Service and was under twenty four hour surveillance.

He knew that his watcher was alone in the club. The rest of the team would have to wait at the end of a gravel path that led from the street, across the park to the clubhouse. Only the single watcher was now in the club.

Mo knew that he had only a limited opportunity to evade MI5. This was that opportunity. He got up and made his way to the toilets. He knew that his watcher was following his every move. He opened the door and entered. He waited.

The wait was not long but felt like hours. After about twelve minutes the watcher was becoming nervous and kept looking at his watch. After sixteen minutes and with Mo not reappearing from the toilet, he had to do something or risk losing his subject.

He made his way past the sofas and tables and pushed the door open. He had waited until he was sure that only his suspect was in the toilets alone. The door swung back. He saw the three doors to the cubicles open and they were empty. There was no one standing at the urinals. In that instant of confusion he lost his life.

Mo had patiently waited just behind the opening door. The watcher for a split second had his back to him. The knife plunged into the side of his neck and the fountain of blood spurted across the white tilled floor. Mo did not wait to see him chock in his own blood but walked immediately from the toilets through the club to the exit. He did not make his way down the gravel drive but climbed through the bordering hedge and walked off across Southgate Park into the night.

****

"You are unbelievable," laughed Madeleine.

"Well some one had to do something. Three thousands agents in MI5, ten addresses for terrorist's cells identified following the surveillance in Luton and not one bugger can get a bug inside any of the locations." said Tim.

"Tim should get an Oscar for his portrayal of old man with heart attack," said Harriet.

"How did you get the ambulance crew to go along with it?"

"We didn't. It was just a gamble. I went outside to meet them and showed them the old MI5 sheriffs badge and asked them to play along and do a bit of medical stuff," said Harriet.

"Risky," said Madeleine.

"Well it worked," said Tim.

"Come on then, what have we found out?" said Harriet.

They were sitting in Tim's office with Madeleine in the Director's chair. Tim was still not passed as fit for work but sitting at home was becoming tedious and so with Harriet's help, he had decided to move matters along in the investigation.

"Here are the transcripts," she pushed a pile of paper across the desk to Tim. She and Harriet had the same information on view on their tablets but she knew that Tim liked things in ink on paper.

There was a few moments silence as they read. Tim spoke first. "I read these as the terrorist cells up and down the Country are expecting a delivery of weapons sometime soon."

"How many individual groups have been identified so far?" said Harriet.

"Well after the MI5 South East Head had the sense to follow the suspect, after his first contact with the occupants at the flat you and Tim bugged yesterday, we think there are nine suspect locations."

"About twenty terrorists plotting something?" said Tim "Have we managed to find out anything more about the suspect, their coordinator, the chap we are calling Mo?"

"He seems to have disappeared, vanished," said Madeleine.

"Hold on," said Harriet. "We are watching a flat in Luton where there are suspected Jihadis. This chap turns up and then makes contacts with other know radicals around the Country and now we don't know where he is?"

Madeleine remained silent for while then spoke. "It is worse. He killed one of our agents in the process."

Tim looked at her. They sat in shocked silence for a moment.

Tim spoke. "Well it is what it is. He could be anywhere. We have to work with what we have, Go back to the surveillance tapes from the Luton flat." He refocused holding back the anger.

They turned their attention back onto the results of Tim and Harriet's bugging. "Well," said Madeleine. "It's pretty clear from the transcripts that they are expecting some sort or weapons delivery."

"What do we do? Watch and wait for the guns or bombs to turn up?"

"I really think that is a bad idea. There is no reason to assume that there will be a knock on the door at these locations and there will be a postman on the door step saying, "good morning Mr Terrorist I have your delivery of Kalashnikovs, please sign here." Is there?" said Tim.

"You're right," agreed Madeleine. "We have precious little to go on though."

"Look we have something we didn't have yesterday. We know that something is imminent and we know that ordinance is on route. We need to look further. The police have been fighting the importation of guns into the UK. The rise in gun crime has made it a hot topic. The tapes seem to imply that our group of terrorists are expecting a delivery of guns and ammunition not bomb making equipment," said Harriet.

"Check with Police and Customs and track back what groups have the ability to come up with the number of guns and ammo that could supply a small army of terrorists," said Madeleine.

"We are not talking a half a dozen hand guns for a few drug dealers here. We are talking an arsenal for a squad of armed Jihadis. The police, Interpol or some agency must have them on the radar somewhere. We just need to look and link it together," said Tim.

Chapter 12

As dusk fell in Chiang Mai the evening air began to turn cool. It was the end of the summer and the beginning of the rainy season. Suzy pulled the shawl up around her shoulders as she stepped from the hotel lobby onto the street. She was surprised at the number of people gathering for the festival of Yi Peng. There were monks, locals and tourists from all around the Globe. All had come to witness the celebrations.

As darkness descended the lanterns would be released. The night sky would be filed with a thousand small suns and the river would become a star covered milky way as the small paper boats were launched, each with its only individual flame. During the weekend there would be dancing, music, parades and fireworks, all in honour of the Buddha.

Suzy had not realised that the festival would be taking place when she had accepted Somchai Onruang's invitation to meet with the Chairman of the Dawar Corporation. She had hoped to meet during the day but Ibrahim had been out of the Country and had only just arrived back. It was decided that they would meet for diner as she was leaving for Bangkok the following day.

She had worked with AGENDA and agencies promoting clean energy and energy reduction for over nine years and knew the score. Money was the driving force. The Dawar corporations of the World were driven by profit with their social conscience directly linked to the size of the grant they could receive form the green agencies.

She knew that her meeting would be less about how Dawar Corporation could operate a cleaner and more energy business and more about the amount of money AGENDA would make available to them. She also knew that in all likelihood a large chunk of the money would go missing in the process redirected to the bank accounts of the officials and company owners participating in the initiative. If ten per cent of the money actually was spent on its intended purpose then that would almost be a success.

The car pulled up outside the hotel. It was late. The driver had struggled to get through the throng of festival goers. He apologised as he opened the rear door to the Mercedes. She settled in the leather seat as the car drove off. She soon realised that Yi Peng may have started as a religious festival but its commercial potential had certainly no been ignored.

Shops were doing a roaring trade selling lanterns to the hordes of tourists who had flocked here. There were advertisements for special dinners with entertainment and river excursions. All and very opportunity was being exploited in an effort to earn the tourist dollar.

There was a large marquee, more a pavilion beside the river. It was festooned by hundreds of lanterns and spot lights lit its façade. A large sign proclaimed Dawar Corporation. She stepped from the limousine onto the red carpet and made her way to the reception line.

It was clear that Dawar were using every opportunity to promote its presence in Thailand. As soon as her feet touched the ground a tuxedo clad man, in his late thirties was at her side. "Welcome, welcome," he enthused taking her hand and shaking it. "My name is Somchai Onruang. You must be Miss Webb?"

Suzy shook the outstretched hand, "Suzy."

"Somchai, please follow me." He offered his arm and led her through the throng of guests. "You are just in time for dinner," he smiled. This was hardly surprising as her car, had been arranged for her by Somchai, who timed the pick up and drop off to coincide with it.

"Please take you place here." He pulled back her chair as she joined the twenty or so guests already seated at the top table. They sat in a long line abreast facing the room full of circular tables each seating ten people. In the centre of the top table sat Ibrahim. Being Pakistani he and she being British stood out from the predominantly Thai guests.

The meal was very palatable and was international in influence rather than wholly Thai. Suzy was surprised that most of her dining companions spoke good English. To her surprise she was enjoying the affair.

The meal was approaching its conclusion when there was the sound of a gong and Ibrahim rose to his feet. "I do not intend to make a long speech. I wish only to welcome you and say thank you for in turn welcoming Dawar to you wonderful Country. On this night of new beginnings and new hope we look forward to continuing success in the future." He raised his glass "prosperity," was the toast.

The word echoed around the marquee as they stood and applauded. "Now let us proceed to the river where we have laid on a little firework display."

Suzy gathered her bag and shawl and got to her feet. She filed to the end of the table following the other guests as they made their way from the dining area. She was intercepted by Somchai. "Please to follow," he said.

They made their way in the opposite direction to the other guests towards the Dawar office building which stood behind the marquee. The security guard recognised Somchai and nodded. He opened the door and Suzy followed Somchai to the lift. "Top floor, Mr Dawar is waiting." He left her alone as the elevator ascended.

The door opened. Ibrahim was expecting her and shook her hand as she exited the lift. She was in a corridor with offices leading off to either side. She followed him to the end where he pushed open a door to the board room. In the centre was a single table large enough for ten or twelve people to sit. It was functional but by no means extravagant. "Please take a seat," he gestured to one of the chairs.

She sat and he walked round to the opposite side and sat facing her

In front of him was a dossier inside a folder bearing the Dawar logo. "Here are our proposals and application. We have committed a great deal of time and thought to the project. My people have examined every aspect of our operations critically to identify key areas where significant impact could be made on the environment. We are confident that AGENDA will be able to see the real contribution we can make to its aims and targets?"

He passed the folder across the table. Suzy sat in silence and began to read. Ibrahim remained silent as she studied the document. On paper the proposal was exactly what her organisation was looking for. It was also self evident that what she was reading had not been prepared by Dawar. The handprint of a well known firm of energy consultants was all over it. She had seen their work time and time again. Knowing that Agenda was handing out money, grants and support in an area, they would approach business in the targeted region and offer their services. Essentially it was no win no fee. They had done the report for Dawar and if successful would receive a healthy share of the money from AGENDA.

Suzy knew that the report would meet every criteria laid down by her agency. Of course what was in the report was likely to bear scant resemblance to the reality. She knew that once the money and credit lines were granted the money was likely as not to disappear into corrupt pockets and very little of it would be applied for the purpose it was intended.

There was no reason and she knew it, to reject the application before her. She felt and air of despondency as she knew little was to change other than the bank balances of the corrupt.

"Very impressive, "she said." It is clear that you have put a great deal of time, effort and consideration into it. On the face of it this would seem the perfect project."

She looked across the table and expected to be greeted with a smiling man who would be reacting like a lottery winner. What looked back at her was the face of a man who might have been told he had terminal cancer.

Ibrahim sat stone still like a statue. His gaze was fixed on her as though she was a ghost raised and walking in the land of the living, He just sat staring straight ahead.

"Are you okay?"

He seemed to come awake and shook himself. There was a slight tremor in his voice as he began to speak. "I am so sorry. It was one of those moments, "he smiled. "I don't know what to say. I did not mean to be rude. What do you say in England?"

"Like a ghost walked over you grave," she volunteered.

"That's it. That is precisely it."

Chapter 13

"Jesus I thought we were done for out there," said Bobby Mortimer.

"You should have more faith in your skipper," came the reply from Neil Kingdom as her pulled the boat alongside the jetty.

"At least that is that last run we have to make." Bobby leapt from the boat and tied off.

There was a flashing of headlights and the sound of an engine starting. The Transit van slowly drove down to where the small cruiser had birthed. Neil joined Bobby and waited as the driver pulled up. Charlie Burns was the brains behind the operation. He and Bobby had been friends since junior school. They lived on the same council estate and started their criminal careers at a young age.

They were bottom feeders in the pond when it came to criminality. They dealt a little weed, pinched car stereos, did a little shop lifting and stole the odd car for a bit of joy riding. Hardly elite gangsters but a constant source of irritation to the local police they would have continued in and out of prison for the rest of their lives but that had changed by chance about eighteen months ago.

Charlie had been smoking a bit of dope with an Afghani in a squat in North London. He had supplied the weed and then decided to have a spiff and a beer with his customer.

"Do you know Jake?" the Afghan had asked as a thick set man came up and sat beside them

"Do you have more?" Jake asked as he joined them. Charlie passed over the dope and Jake handed over the money. He rolled up and a conversation started between the men.

"Jake got me into the Country." The Afghan said by way of introduction. "He's a rich man."

"The fuck I am," said Jake. From his accent it was clear to Charlie that Jake was some sort of Eastern European, Romanian or Albanian. "I get nothing the guys in Calais get the real dough. I just meet the trucks and sort you out this end."

Charlie was always up for making money and his interest was aroused. "How much did you pay to get here then?"

"Fifteen thousand euros for the trip."

"What from Afghanistan to England?" asked Charlie?

"Like bollocks they dumped me at Calais."

"So how did you get across the Channel?"

"I tried all the usual like sneaking in the back of a truck. I made it to the UK quite a few times but got caught at Customs here and sent back to France. It's hard man. They know all the tricks and catch most of us."

"So how did you make it?"

"More money, more fucking money, my family scrapped it together and sent it, then a small boat across into a small harbour with no customs. It is the best way. They cannot watch every bit of coast."

Charlie was soon talking to Neil, who had a boat. It was all he had left of his inheritance. Unlike Charlie and Bobby he was posh, public school posh but he was also a junkie. His Mother had died when he was very young and when his Dad passed it had not taken him long to work his way through the inheritance. He and Charlie's paths had crossed when they shared a prison ceil. Neil never sold the boat. It was called Melinda after his mother. It was the only link he had to her so he never sold it no matter how bad things got.

With introductions from Jake they, Charlie, Bobby and Neil soon found their way into the people smuggling business. Surprisingly Neil was actually a very good sailor. It was not the career path his father had intended when he had paid out for his expensive education but he was at least putting some of it to good use now.

They were all now making good money but it was risky. It was only a matter of time before the coast guard, the police or the customs bagged them. They knew it. They had a number of close run ins with the authorities but had been lucky so far. They knew that their luck could not hold forever.

There was also the distinct possibility of ending up at the bottom of the English Channel. Taking a small boat rammed to gunnels with illegal immigrants, in the dark with no lights showing, across the busiest shipping lanes in the World was not without danger. If they were not run over by a ship, the sea North Sea was quite capable of sinking them on its own without any help from the maritime fleet.

"Deux pression," said Neil to the waiter in the café in Calais.

"Smart arse," said Charlie," Mr posh boy speaking your school boy French."

They were sat outside a bar in the centre of the town. They made regular trips to buy booze and cigarettes. They were sort of recognised as petty customs duty evaders by the authorities, stretching their personal drink and tobacco allowances to the limit. It was a sort of double bluff while they made other trips in the dead of night with their cargo of illegal immigrants.

The beer arrived and they sat smoking watching the people. When the tide turned they would make their way back with their duty reduced cargo. They become aware of a group of three men paying them an unusual amount of attention. When they had entered the café there had been only one party interested in them. He had made a phone call and was now joined by two others. They sat looking at Charlie and Neil while a discussion took place between them. Obviously a decision had been made and one of their group stood up and approached them.

"May I sit?" he did not wait for a reply and sat.

Charlie looked at Neil and raised an eyebrow. They were wary of their uninvited guest. The three studied each other closer and there was a moments silence before the new arrival spoke. "I think we may have business in common."

"You're a window cleaner, as well?"

The man looked confused not being ready for the famous British sense of humour, "Ah a joke?"

"Look mate we don't know what you're selling but we're not buying today," said Charlie. Charlie had muscle as well as a brain and he had learned the hard way how to handle himself. Unlike Neil he had learned how to fight at an early age and was not afraid of a bit of extreme violence when required.

The man realising he was in danger of being hospitalised at any moment raised his hands, palms outwards in a gesture of placation and said," just a talk. We may have something that interests you."

That had been three weeks earlier. Now they found themselves back in England in the dead of night with a boat loaded with enough guns and explosives to start a small war. In the intervening period they had made four trips smuggling the supplies for the various terrorist cells readying themselves. Tonight was the last of their cargo. They would drive them to the rented lockup garage and stash them with the rest of their haul. Tomorrow they would be contacted and the arms would be collected. Then they would be in the money, real money for once and the Country would face the biggest terrorist threat in a decade.

Chapter 14

Somchai Onruang was feeling the tension in the truck as they made there way through the jungle of Myanmar to the Hukawng Valley. This was a war zone. The war has raged for years between the Northern Alliance, comprising armed ethnics groups wanting independence and the Burmese military, the Tatmadaw. They were on route to the secret location of the KIA, a group of Christian insurgents.

"Why can't they just move the Jade across the border into China in the normal way? If this Xi is in so tight with the Chinese military it shouldn't be a problem. The whole area around Hpakant is under Tatmadaw control now. They drove the KIA out in the 1990s." said Somchai.

"That's his problem. The Chinese military elite have total control in the region through their connections with their counterparts in Myanmar. They are carving up the Jade trade between them. It's a monopoly. Xi acts as a broker and picks up the crumbs as a middle man. It is precarious. In China you can be part of the elite one day and in a prison the next as the President pushes on to become Dictator for life," said Ibrahim. The discussion had taken place on Ibrahim's return from his trip to Macau.

"If they have the area under control where is this Jade coming from that we are supposed to get to China?"

"The KIA managed to stockpile it before being driven out of the mines. They are sitting on billions of dollars worth of it. They need guns. And they need the money to finance their war against the Tatmadaw. Their customers are in China but the Chinese won't buy from them."

"The Myanmar and Chinese Generals have craved up the trade between them and don't want upset the apple cart."

"Exactly, they are sitting on fortune with no way of cashing in on it. That is where we and our Chinese friends come in," said Ibrahim. "We have a license to export Jade from Pakistan to China, cheap nephrite jade. Xi is officially importing that but we are going to swap it en route for top quality jadeite worth billions."

"All we have to do is get the jade from the KIA in Burma. Bring it across the border into Thailand and substitute it for the crap you have put on the boat from Pakistan," said Somchai.

What had seemed easy in a conversation in a comfy office in Chiang Mai was in reality now a journey through hell. The mines were like a trip into underworld. The precious stone was concentrated in the foothills of the Himalayas. On paper the Government licensed the operations and the mines but in reality the area was sealed off and run by the military.

The mines were mostly illegal and the Government received none of the proceeds. The area was locked down by the military. It was off limits and therefore beyond scrutiny and regulation. It was a modern Wild West ruled by the gun.

The Chinese fuelled the trade providing the capital and bribing the Tatmadaw and the Myanmar officials. They carved into the mountains day and night mining the ore, scarring the landscape and destroying the jungle and everything before them.

The poor and the needy scavenged the tailings piles. Vast mountains of rubble covered the landscape tuning it into an alien planet. A vast no mans land, inhabited by grey impoverished figures that toiled under the yoke of an unforgiving and uncaring master. Greed drove the inhumane conditions and it was a veracious predator. It cared nothing for the environment. It cared less for the wildlife and it cared even less for human life.

The lust for Jade sacrificed any notion of humanity. The official workers were no more than salves to be used, ground up and spat out. On the peripheral there was an army of ghostly grey figures that scrabbled in the dirt, for the cast offs of the mining companies.

Hour after hour, day after day, day and night the massive dumper trucks would wend their way to the top of the mounds of dirt and rubble to unload the tailings from the extraction process. These vast mountains of slag were home to a vast barely surviving army of scavengers.

Each time a truck emptied its load there would be a rush to pick through the discard. From a distance it looked like a vast colony of ants was swarming over the huge mountains of loose stone and rubble. They seemed to appear in the mist like phantoms in their hundreds from nowhere, swarm the tips and then rush to the next as another truck unloaded.

They died, were maimed and injured in the frequent land slides. The vast mounds were unstable. The trucks kept dumping building the heap bigger and bigger. The tailings would settle naturally by shifting and creating sudden and massive landslides. Boulders would roll down the tips crushing and burying those picking through the discard.

No one cared. The mining was relentless. The ore was dug from the mines. Rock and Jade were separated. The trucks dumped the tailings. The price on the land and the people was ignored. Jade ruled all. It consumed all and it would be so as long as there was any left to mine.

There shanty towns were the place of business for the Chinese Jade dealers. They would buy from the scavengers of the rubble heap. They would come carrying rock large and small, the leftovers, hands and feet torn and bleeding from hours crawling and scrabbling on the vast mounds. The buyers would gather and bid for the ore. There were no guarantees. There was a constant whiff of violence that hung in the air. Fights and quarrels were a constant backdrop.

The sellers would scurry off clutching their meagre rewards, another day of life and food for their family. The buyers would anxiously inspect their purchase. There were no guarantees. What looked a promising rock and had fetched a high price when opened could contain little of none of the precious gemstone of worth. Colour and flawlessness was all. It determined what the carvers could use, the size and beauty of the final piece. In the hands of the best craftsmen in China these rocks obtained with such pain and suffering would become the most beautiful works of art, some almost priceless.

The trucks came to a halt. "We are here." said the guide the KIA had provided.

Somchai looked around nervously. "I don't see anyone."

"They will be here. You must wait."

He did not like the wait. His nerves were at breaking point. With the guide's help they had avoided the Myanmar military. They had been off road for most of the long and arduous journey. The trucks had started journey loaded with barrels of diesel. They were now empty. They had created their own supply drops for the return journey. The trucks would be loaded with tons of Jade and would drive from dump to dump to fuel their journey back to the Thai border.

Somchai knew that this was only the beginning. The next phase was to transport the Jade to the port in Thailand and substitute it for the virtually worthless Pakistani nephrite. Ibrahim had eased the process with the necessary bribes that were a requirement of any smooth business transaction in the Country. That of course depended on him getting back alive.

"There, see, over there," their guide pointed down the valley.

He could see nothing at first. Gradually a small group of rebels came into view. It was a further full hour before they actually marched up and surrounded the trucks.

Somchai nervously stepped down from the cab and hailed the group. They acknowledged the guide but ignored him and his drivers. They were suspicious. They had learned to be so. They had no air force and so were always susceptible from attack from the skies by the Tatmadaw. They were losing ground and desperately needed the arms that this deal would finance. What they did not need was their location being exposed and attacked.

They began a thorough search of the trucks for any form of tracking device. He and the drivers had been warned that any mobile phones found on them would result in their immediate execution. They all had taken the warning seriously and left them behind. It was far too easy to track a phone signal.

Satisfied the rebels boarded the trucks and began to guide them to the rendezvous point. It was a further three and a half hours of driving through rough terrain before a halt was called. He could see nothing. He inspected the barren hillside looking for the precious cargo, "Where?" he said.

The guide smiled and the rebels began to disembark. Somchai followed the guide to the rocky hillside. "Here," he said.

It was so well camouflaged that standing right next to the diesel powered fork lift, he had not seen it until he nearly fell over it. The jade was stacked in plain view all around. They set to work loading the trucks.

Chapter 15

The Hi Si club was like nothing she had ever seen before. Suzy had enjoyed her evening at Dawar's invitation and after their meeting she had returned to the party. After a few drinks she was in the mood for local colour of a different variety than floating lanterns.

"Hi my name is Elise. You look so beautiful I felt I should say hello," the young Thai woman was brazen in her approach. Suzy could not deny that she was stunningly beautiful. She was surprised that this woman had picked upon her sexuality so quickly. Perhaps there was some truth that homosexuals could recognise each other with some sort of built in radar. She had never had that talent herself. She dismissed the thought and concentrated on her new companion.

"Suzy," she held out her hand. Elise took it and gently stroked it, leaving her in no doubt that there was interest there, before letting go.

Suzy has struggled with her sexuality for years, unhappy years in denial before she had accepted who she was. Her life had finally come together when she had joined the police. She had a partner, nearly ten years older than her but she was in love, she had stability, a career and a home life.

It had all gradually disintegrated after the shooting at the Mosque. Now many years ago it still remained but life moves on and people change. She now avoided long term commitment and settled on a life with no complications. Perhaps it was a mid-life crisis or perhaps she just wanted to have fun.

Elise seemed to tick the no complication fun box. She began to flirt wit her unashamedly. She did not stop to wonder why the young beauty seemed so eager. Perhaps it was the drink or perhaps she was just feeling randy, whatever the reason caution was being thrown to the wind.

Most businessmen and women of any experience are well versed in the probability of being honey trapped by the competitors or by associates. In a high profile organisation like AGENDA she knew that being compromised was always a possibility and sex was mostly the carrot and then subsequently the stick of first choice.

Not illegal but still a silly position to get into. These days in the West the threat of being blackmailed for being a homosexual seemed irrelevant. Of course not all countries had that same outlook and it still remained a major crime around the globe. Thailand however had a very liberal view of sex. Perhaps that disarmed her but she should have known better. It could be easily misinterpreted as an inducement to give Dawar's application favourable treatment. Suzy did not consider it as she spoke to her new found friend.

"Perhaps we could go on somewhere," she suggested.

Suzy had taken little persuading and soon they were pulling up outside the HI Si club. They stepped from the taxi onto the pavement. As the cab drove away Suzy asked, "Hi Si?"

"High Society, it is a club for the more affluent. You will see." They made their way inside. The doorman seemed to know Elsie.

It was nothing like Suzy had expected. In fact she was not sure what she had expected. It was not a bar or a night club. The furnishings were lavish but more like a lounge, comfy sofas, chairs and television screens on the wall. It was more an extension of the home for the well heeled in Thai society. Both sexes were represented amongst the guests. Expensively dressed men and women patrons mixed with obvious prostitutes, male escorts and lady boys.

The transsexuals were stunningly beautiful. Suzy found it impossible to distinguish them from the beautiful female prostitutes. There was no difference except they had a penis but apart from that they were for intents and purposes beautiful women.

She sat on a sofa for two with her companion. Champagne arrived and Suzy was in no doubt she would be paying for it. She did not mind. They toasted and soon she was gently embracing and kissing her companion.

She was one of a few westerners in the club. The locals seemed to have no sexual hang-ups. The well dressed women would openly disappear up the stairs hand in hand with a young gigolo and the men would do the same. It was the norm here. It was liberating for Suzy who spent so much time in her job in Countries with regimes that were repressive. Even in the West sex was not this open and easily available.

"Shall we take a room?" said Elise.

"Why not?"

She followed her up the staircase. The upstairs was like a five star hotel, well decorated, lavish and subdued lighting. It exuded romance. The room was fashionable with a king-sized bed in pride of place.

"Sit," her companion commanded.

Elise picked up the remote controller and soft music began to play from the concealed speakers in the room. She had obviously done this many times before. The rooms in the HI Si club were familiar and part of her normal routine.

Suzy watched as she began to gyrate sensually to the music. It was subtle, erotic not raunchy. She starred directly into Suzy's eyes holding her gaze as he slowly began to remove her clothing. It was enthralling. Elise was employing the skills she had learned in the bars to entice and excite.

She removed her dress sliding it slowly to the ground. She wore no bra and her breast bore slight scars underneath where they had been enhanced. The nipples were hard and very dark against the pale olive smoothness of her skin. She reached up raising her hands above her head and danced slowly side to side her entire body offering the promise of sex to come.

She laughed and then jumped up and down bouncing her breasts then moved side to side causing them to rotate slightly, "Another drink?" The sudden change from sultry to playful made Suzy laugh as well. Elise was expert at building expectation and then interjecting humour. She would tease her audience deferring their gratification and building desire.

It was working. Suzy wanted her. It became almost unbearable as Elise turned her back and made her way to the champagne bucker. She swayed her bottom from side to side as she poured the drinks. Suzy was transfixed by the perfect rear end of her new found companion. She knew that she was being seduced and she did not care. Her desire was overriding her reasoning. She was living in the moment.

"Drink," the glass was placed in her hand. They linked arms and made a lover's toast. "Drink it all then we shall fuck until we drop."

For a moment Suzy hesitated slightly shocked by the coarseness of her companion. She was in Thailand and not the Home Counties and their approach to sex was open and direct. She felt a secret thrill at her own boldness. "Fuck to we drop," she replied and drank the champagne down in one.

Elise began raised herself up and began to dance again. Suzy remembered her panties siding down and the small triangle of black pubic hair, then nothing.

It was dark when she struggle through a thick mist into consciousness. She was disoriented, confused and her head was pounding. Had she passed out? Had she had sex with this beautiful Thai girl? Was it morning? She opened her eyes and expected to find herself in bed with her companions long black hair draped across the pillow beside her. There was no pillow. There was no soft black hair. There was no bed.

She tried to sit up and get her bearings. She tried to raise herself onto one elbow but she could not move. She could not move her legs.

She could not move her arms. She felt the panic rise. For an instant she thought she was paralysed. She screamed and opened her eyes.

She realised she was completely naked and tied in a heavy wooden chair, in the middle of a bare of crudely plastered warehouse. The bright neon light burned into her brain as she tried to focus on her surroundings. The most illogical thought given her situation jumped into her mind. "Don't you realise how energy inefficient and wasteful neon is?"

"That is the least of your worries Ms Webb," came the reply.

Chapter 16

2007

It was so little to show for a life, a small brown paper wrapped parcel. It sat in the middle of the table as the light faded in the village in Pakistan. He sat looking at it. He had looked at it for nearly a week. Opening it would have meant acceptance, acceptance that life had changed forever. Opening it would be to acknowledge that all that would remain would be memories.

He knew he could not delay the evitable for ever. The grief and loss could not be avoided but it was all so final. A few short months ago his wife and daughter, his only child and her mother had boarded a plane for England. It was to be the most joyous moment for him, his daughter was to marry. It would be a new chapter in their lives. There was a future filled with new beginnings in a new Country.

How could it end in a small parcel sitting on a table? It was so little for so much hope. Could lives really be reduced to some ashes and a small box? How had it come to this?

Mina had returned to the Coroner's Court. The verdict was to be announced. She, Sami and Reza linked hands as the reading began. She knew from the opening sentence what the Coroner would find but when it was delivered in the calm, clear and dispassionate voice hearing it cut to her soul.

"We completely exonerate the police and commend them on their actions in defending this Country against the evil threat posed by these terrorists who seek only the destruction of our democratic way of life." The Coroner concluded.

Her daughter had been murdered. It was all one big lie. The police had painted her beautiful innocent child as some sort of crazed terrorist who had come to England with the sole purpose of murder. She has come full of hope and excitement her heart filled with love for her to be husband, Reza. She was just looking for a better life, a future the chance to bring up her children. There was no hatred or murder in her heart.

"Are you okay?" said Sami.

Mina could say nothing.

Reza said, "We need to get out of here."

His mother and Mina rose from their seats. They were in shock. They looked at Reza and failed to understand his agitation.

"We need to get out of here right now," he said urgently. He pulled his mother to her feet, "Auntie, come on."

In a daze Mina followed them from the room into the vestibule. It was crowded and Reza pushed his way through and created a gap for his mother and aunt to follow as he parted the bodies in their way. They reached the large door that led to the street beyond.

What followed was a haze. Mina was in a world far away enveloped in grief and disbelief. Nothing could prepare her for what lay beyond the Courthouse door. She stepped into a hell of flashing camera lights, milling reporters, screaming questions and a police cordon.

The road was blocked with hundreds of shouting people. The mood was intimidating and hysterical. The atmosphere was hostile. People screamed and waved placards. "Pakis go home", Death to Muslims". They were spat at, sworn at and manhandled as the police escorted them to a waiting cab.

They finally reached the door of the taxi. It was held open by a young police woman. They squeezed though the protesters and managed to reach the safety of the back of the vehicle. As she closed the door the PC added one final word," scum," she sneered as she pushed the door shut.

Javeria body was released and the family could at last carry out the funerary rights. Mina tried to console herself that her daughter was in a better place. She looked for comfort in her faith. She could not find it. All she could see was the injustice and the distortion of her memory. The story was too good and sold newspapers. "Jihadi brides come to England to Kill," was the theme they adopted.

Mina sunk into a deeper and deeper depression as the truth was further and further distorted. Her daughter had been shot in cold blood for no reason by a policewoman who was being hailed as a hero. She played the footage on the phone, the footage of her daughter's killer being guarded by her colleagues and safely taken from the Court to carry on her life while her daughter was gone.

For Suzy it had been a moment of panic and lack of experience. For the police it was a combination of poor intelligence, poor planning and lack of proper command and control. She wanted to admit her mistake. She felt the guilt weighing on her. That could not be allowed to happen. Careers were at stake. It was not the narrative being pushed by police and politicians. Reputations needed to be maintained and public confidence restored in an inadequate and poorly organised and institutional racist police force. They could not afford more scandal.

Suzy had panicked. She had waited at the scene denying access to all, including her partner that day Charles. She had followed the instructions in her ear. She watched as the gun was planted in Javeria's hand. She waited until the scene of crime forensics team arrived. The cover up was complete.

For Suzy it was just the beginning of the guilt. "I have to tell the truth," she had said. She was at home in the arms of her partner.

"You know that cannot happen. It is done now. Think of our life together," had been the reply.

Suzy left the police and left her lover. She had to live with herself and her conscience but she did not have to live with the constant reminders of it. She made a new life for herself with AGENDA.

There was no new life for Mina. Her life was over. She could not bring herself to return to her life and husband in Pakistan. Her life was bound in the cold and windy Country where her daughter had been killed.

Reza was struggling with life. He had seen his life in terms of his work and the future with Javeria. He had never been a deeply devout Muslim. The desire to fit in and progress in Britain had on occasions led him form the path of Islam. He had adjusted and become pragmatic. Now he realised, that path had been wrong. He saw that God had punished him. He had strayed from the path of the Prophet and his future happiness had been wiped away by the gunshots that day in the Mosque.

He found his faith amidst his despair. His devotion grew and grew. He attended the teachings and preaching of the more radical clerics. His eyes were opened to the truth. He had what the authorities liked to call, been radicalised. He however saw it has having his eyes opened to the oppression of his brothers by the unbelievers.

Mina woke that morning some five weeks after the verdict and dressed. It was early morning and cold as she made her way to Stratford underground station. The early morning commute was underway and the platform crowded as she made her way along it. They trains were packed but running on time. They would not continue to run on time.

She heard the approach of the next train and felt the blast of wind rush along the platform as the air in front of it was pushed from the tunnel. She jumped. She landed on the live rail and was electrocuted just as the wheels sliced through her body.

Her husband, finally unwrapped the parcel that Sami, his sister in law had posted to him. Then he tipped its meagre contents onto the table. A watch, some bangles and a photo Mina had taken with her to England, of their wedding day. There was so little to remind him of her.

There was nothing of his daughter at all. He had last seen his wife and daughter as they had boarded at train. They had never come back just a little cardboard box of oddments had been returned in their place.

There was one final small box wrapped in a note. He pulled the elastic band off and freed the note wrapped around the Nokia mobile box.

The note was in Sami's handwriting. "The phone was a present to Mina from Reza. I think there are some photos on it of Javeria."

Chapter 17

"How do you like the new technology?" said Madeleine.

"Can we get the cricket?" said Tim. He, Harriet and Madeleine were in the control room at MI5 headquarters. An array of videos screens displayed events taking place in real time relayed from operations in the field.

"I just could not believe you got the funding for all this," said Harriet.

"It is an amazing achievement. The stuff we were working with was creaking at the seams. Harriet and I tried to convince everyone that we needed state of the art equipment and got nowhere. How did you manage it?" said Tim.

Madeleine looked pleased at the praise. "It was not easy. In a way what happened to you was the extra grain of sand that tipped the scaled and opened the purse. You were out in the field and we were down to using mobile phones to communicate with you and the police."

"Not state of the art by a long chalk," said Harriet.

"Pathetic really," continued Madeleine. "At one point we lost contact with the police, you and GCHQ. We couldn't even get a fix on the phones locations owing to the lack of coverage, madness for a Country's security service, total insanity."

"How does it work?" asked Tim.

"You're asking that? You really want to know? Bear in mind you struggle to set the alarm on your mobile phone," laughed Harriet.

"That's a little harsh. I can text in lower case now and put a smiley face at the end."

"Progress indeed," said Madeleine.

"Come," persisted Tim. "Tell me how it works."

"We have our own, satellite, servers, software and closed network that links everything from traffic lights to body cams …"

"You're right. I don't really want to know."

Madeleine and Harriet both laughed. "Well that went well," said Madeleine.

"So what's on the telly?" said Tim.

Bobby Mortimer. Neil Kingdom Charlie Burns were totally unaware that they were under surveillance. They had been for four months. The French Police watched as they left the café in Calais. The phones calls between their new found arms dealing friends had immediately attracted their attention. Intelligence had led them from the dealer to them and from them hopefully to the money. They would then follow the money and the arms to the terrorist in England.

The rain was falling has the loaded the last of their cargo into the hired truck. "Come on, we need to get a shift on," said Bobby.

"I need to make sure the boat is secure before we leave. It won't take a moment," said Neil.

"He does love that boat, doesn't he," said Charlie.

"I hope I never see the bloody thing again. I was not cut out for bobbing about on the Ocean blue malarkey, I bleeding hate it," said Bobby.

Neil finished messing around aboard the boat and eventually climbed in the cab along side his companions. "What the fuck is that?"

"An uzi pistol," he smiled.

"Are you mental? What in God's name are you going to do with that?"

"It's cool."

"He's a real gangster now," said Charlie as he drove up the ramp and left the harbour. They first of the surveillance teams picked them up. The cars would swap order and change as the convoy progressed to the warehouse where the rest of the arsenal was already stored.

They were completely unaware that their every move had been watched from day one. The French police were posed and ready to arrest their contacts there. It would be a co-ordinated operation on both sides of the Channel. This was to ensure that the suspects could not contact and warn each other that they had been busted.

Just under two hours later, at just gone 3 am the truck pulled up at the warehouse in an industrial estate near Enfield Lock in North London. The police were already in situ, hidden in cars and vans minutes from the unit.

"That was a drive and a half," said Booby.

"What did you want me to do? Speeding at this time of the morning would just be a red flag to a bull. The rozzers would have us over faster than you could fart."

"I know it's just that my arse has gone numb."

"Stop talking. We need to get the gear inside," said Charlie.

"Can't we just leave it in the van and when they turn up move it to theirs along with the stuff in the lock up?"

"No we bleeding can't. Get the van emptied. Drive it off the estate and come back in the car. The less activity the less chance of anyone getting nosey. Someone might see the van and think there's a blag going down and call the filth. Now move it."

After a considerable amount of moaning the guns were inside, the van was parked a good distance away and the three of them were waiting for the arrival of their customers. The police were waiting as well and Tim, Madeleine and Harriet were watching the progress on the direct feed to MI5.

"What are you doing?" Charlie asked.

"Having a little lift," Bobby and Neil lit the meth pipe. They were soon high. Charlie knew this was not good but what could he do. Two meth heads and a pile of guns. This was not in his planning.

Mo waited in a side street a mile away. He had seen them return with the last of the guns. He was in no rush. Now was not the time for rashness. When he was sure that there was no threat he would approach the estate, check the cargo, and load it aboard his van. He would transfer the money on his iPad. Then he would set off on a trip around the Country and deliver to the terrorist cells waiting to go into action.

He was sure that it was clear. He stated the engines and drove into the estate. This he knew was the critical point. Once he made contact and the arms were in his possession that would be when he would be most vulnerable.

He pulled the van to a halt. All was quiet. He waited and finally the roll up door was raised by Charlie. Mo moved into the light. "Jeez man, what the fuck?"

It was clear that Neil and Booby were completely off their faces. "Let's just get It done," said Charlie.

The two laboured to move the crates from the lock up to Mo's Van. Bobby made an ineffectual attempt to give them a hand but he and Neil were too wired to be of any real use. Their agitation and hyper activeness was making matters difficult and noisy. It was also distracting, so distracting that they were caught unprepared.

"Armed police, armed police," the area was suddenly alive with police coming from all directions. Mo and Charlie dropped to their knees in compliance with the shouted commands.

"That seems to have gone off as planned," said Madeleine as they watched the feed from the body cams.

"We need to raid the cells countrywide and mop them up," said Tim.

The sound of gunfire suddenly filled the night. Neil and Booby ran from the lock up. They held an Uzi in each hand and were firing in all directions. At 600 hundred rounds a minute it was a hailstorm of lead flying in all directions. Police were being hit and dying as Madeleine, Harriet and Tim sat watching in their executive chairs.

Then chaos as the police ran for cover. The two wannabe gangsters, high, irrational stood firing their guns. The police armed response unit regrouped. Their fire was deadly accurate. Bobby was hit simultaneously by several marksmen. They were head shots. Having seen their colleagues gunned down they were in no mood to wound. He died, his head almost disintegrated. Neil seemed to have a moment of clarity and tried to put his weapons down, too little too late. He too was brought down by a deluge of police gun fire.

Charlie and the terrorist known to MI5 as Mo lay on the ground. The police broke cover and advanced cautiously their attention focussed on Neil and Bobby's bodies watching for any sign of movement. Their priority was to ensure that the immediate threat was eradicated

"Jesus, what a fuck up," said Madeleine as they watched the wounded and dead police. It was mayhem, an operation gone badly wrong.

"It seems under control now," commented Harriet.

They could see the tension go from the bodies of the advancing police as they approached Mo and Charlie. There was an almost euphoric atmosphere among those not injured, a relief at having survived a battle and lived.

Without warning the screens went white. It was a flash of such intensity that it was like a bolt of lightening illuminating the control room. "What happened?"

"Jesus Christ, the van was rigged with explosives. It must have exploded," screamed Tim.

As the smoke cleared and the cameras adapted the picture appeared. The van driven by Mo was no more. A crater had appeared. The lock up and surroundings building were now a pile of rubble. Stunned figurers were stumbling around confused and shocked. The injured and dying were moaning and crying out for help. The dead were silent.

Chapter 18

"Where I am?" asked Suzy.

"Does it matter? All you need to know is that it's payback time you bitch."

It was a foggy haze. She tried to recall how she had got here. She remembered the Marquee, a meeting with the head of the Dawar Corporation, a beautiful Thai woman, a club, a bedroom, champagne and a bed. The champagne, how could she have been so stupid? She had been drugged.

"Let me go," she struggled against the restraints keeping her in the chair.

"That is not going to happen. I have waited a long time for this."

"What are you going to do to me?"

"Why kill you of course."

"Why, why?" she was hysterical, crying and fighting to move. The slap was powerful and unexpected. Her head was knocked to the side and blood filled her mouth,

"Shut up."

She couldn't. She became more hysterical. This time a punch to her face broke her nose, her top teeth were loosened. "Now do I have your attention?"

Suzy shook uncontrollably and felt the urine run down her legs as she sat uncomprehending in agony. For good measure without warning she was punched in the stomach, leaving her gasping for breath. She sat whimpering, terrified.

"Are you sitting comfortably," there was a sneering half laugh as her tormentor continued to speak. "Then I shall begin. Once upon a time there was a beautiful young girl. Her mother and her father loved her dearly and she grew up to be a beautiful young women. She was clever as well as beautiful."

"Her parents were not rich but they did their best to give her a good and happy life. The years passed and the time came for her to marry and have a family of her own. It was important to her mother and father that they found just the right man for her. They had no other children. Allah in his infinite wisdom had only blessed them with a daughter. She was the most precious gift."

He stepped forward and punched Suzy again. "Are you someone's precious gift?"

She said nothing struggling through the pain.

"No I think not. You are an abomination, a sinner in the eyes of God, a fornicator with your own sex. You are vile and disgusting yet you live." He took several deep breaths and resumed his tale.

"They consulted and they searched their hearts for a suitable husband. It was important that he had faith. That he was a good and devout Muslim and a good and kind man. Such men are hard to find. The World is full of sinners and philanderers."

"It was decided upon and a husband was chosen. There was joy and there was sadness, a father would lose a daughter and young man would gain a bride. She would have to travel many miles away to a new land to be with her betrothed and her parents saved and sold much of what they had to pay for her air fare."

"The day came and her father wept as she left with her mother and her aunt for the flight to England. There was not enough money for him to go with them but he was happy and filled with hope for a better life for his dear daughter."

"He delighted to hear from his daughter. She phoned to tell him she was in love. She was excited and found in her fiancée that all she could have wished for. She was finding England very different to her life in Pakistan. It was all new. It was an adventure. She was so alive with the wonder of it all."

Suzy knew at that point that this was the moment in her life that she knew she would have to confront at some time. In a way it was a relief, a release. One instant in time, one action, and one choice had altered everything. A decision taken in a blur of panic had redefined her as a human being. She had often tried to absolve herself, a lack of training, a lack of intelligence, a lack of planning and a failing in the command and control structure danced through her mind in attempted justification.

There was no real absolution. The plain and simple truth was she had taken the decision on herself to enter that room. She should have waited. She should have warned those behind that door. She should not have panicked. She should not have discharged her gun into a room full of women and children. She should not have killed a young bride to be.

Her tormentor seemed to sense her desolation. "You should have protected his daughter, his innocent and pure daughter. You chose instead to put a bullet in her head."

He continued. "Her father waited for news of the wedding, the guests, the celebrations and the union. He was alone thousands of miles away when he heard that his daughter had been shot."

"He was not a stupid man. He knew that there were bad people out there. People who twisted the words of God to there own ends. He may have understood that his precious daughter had been accidentally killed, an innocent casualty like so many others. He knew that there was no evil in her heart. So heartbroken he waited on British justice to restore the honour to her memory."

Suzy felt the hatred and agony in the next blow that struck her. "He did not get any of that. The World was instead told that his daughter was a terrorist, a Jihadi bent on killing. She had travelled to England with the aim of murder. There she had armed herself. She had conspired to go out and slaughter."

"He could not understand. This was not the kind loving daughter he knew. Her last conversation had been full of happiness over her impending marriage. How was it possible that in the space of twenty four hours she had become a gun carrying terrorist?"

"It was only possible in your mind Ms Webb. You not only murdered her in cold blood you set about defiling her memory, to save yourself. You killed her. You put the gun in her hand. You lied in court. You murdered her twice."

"A mother sat and listened to the lies you told. She was in the room when you hid your shame behind a screen, protected from view. You could lie with no eyes upon you. You could smirk in satisfaction while you defiled her memory. You could walk free and live your life."

"Others now had no life and no memories. Her mother had lost the thing she held most dear. She would see no wedding day, no rejoicing and hope for the future. There would be no marriage, no life and no grandchildren, gone in an instant with a quick burst of gunfire."

"You destroyed so many lives and it continued. Her mother had no reason to continue. She was the cause of major disruption on the underground system when she jumped in front of a train."

"Her father was left alone. He only had the hope that one day Allah would bring him justice."

"You are going to die Miss Webb but before you die you have the chance to put right an in justice. You will tell me who helped you. You could not have done this alone. Some one covered up for you. Some one tampered with evidence. Some one put that gun in my daughter's hand."

Her screams could not be heard deep in the solitude of the Thai countryside. She died. She died but not before she condemned others.

Jade

She gave up the name.

Chapter 19

General Xi waited nervously for the phone call. He knew he was playing a dangerous game but the rewards were great, greater than the risk he was taking. For years he had played second fiddle to his better connected masters, the elite that were in favour and were granted license to build vast fortunes for themselves as long as they toed the line.

They were worth billions. They had moved their money from China around the globe. They and the fellow kleptocrats mostly Russian, formed shell companies to buy up top real estate in New York and London. But Xi knew time was running out. The president, Xi Jinping was consolidating his power into a dictatorship. The old corrupt elite were being systematically targeted and disposed of. It was only a matter of time before his masters were wiped away and he along with them.

This was his big play. The pay off that would set him free for life. He had his plans to get himself out and take his family. It now all depended on one shipment from Pakistan via Thailand. He had spoken to Ibrahim. He knew the Jade had been retrieved from Myanmar and successfully substituted for the worthless nephrite. He had the permits. He had paid the bribes. He needed to know that it was now in Hong Kong heading to his Chinese buyers.

They had paid half up front. That money was gone. He had used that to pay the KIA rebels in Myanmar. He would receive the balance on safe delivery. Then and only then would he be able to breath safely. If something went wrong now there was no way back. They would not be forgiving. He would die and so would his family.

The phone rang. A few words and he sat back in his chair and exhaled loudly. It had cleared customs and they had taken delivery. He was a very rich man. His money awaited him in the Cayman islands, the true ownership concealed behind layers of shell companies and fake identities established by Panamanian lawyers. He just had to go and collect.

He considered not paying Ibrahim his cut. Greed is a great driver. He weighed his options. True there was little the man could do. He could not take the matter to the courts. However he could expose Xi to the Chinese government. He decided that it was not worth the gamble. He picked up the phone.

"The package has arrived," Xi said.

"I am aware of that and I have been waiting for your call," replied Ibrahim.

Xi knew he had been right to honour their agreement. The threat was implicit. Ibrahim had been tracking the jade. He knew that Xi had it. He could with one call expose Xi's duplicity and ensure his arrest and eventual death.

"I am just ringing to confirm that payment will be on its way within the hour."

There was a silence. It was clear that there was more to be said. Xi could not imagine what that was but he waited for Ibrahim to speak. "Things have changed for me."

"Changed, changed how, the matter is surely concluded?"

"It is but I am willing to take far less than agreed, a sort of swap."

Xi was uncomfortable. "I don't understand."

"I want something that you may be in a position to deliver. It is worth far less than you owe me."

The phone call finished. Xi had let greed get the better of him. It was a risk, a big risk but it was also a lot of money he would save by not paying Ibrahim. He tried not to be superstitious. He did not want to fit the Chinese stereotype but he knew that this just had to be auspicious. It was fate.

Only ten days before he had been tasked by his commander to oversee and test the very item Ibrahim asked if he could acquire for him. He got up from his desk and looked from his window. It was madness, total madness.

The more he thought about the more simple he realised it was. His orders were clear. He was to secretly deploy and test them. It would only take his order and signature to do as Ibrahim had requested. He knew he would be found out but he planned to be long gone before that.

He picked up the internal phone. "Come in now. I have some orders to be sent."

****

Mo, as he was called by MI5, lay on the ground. The police were focussed on the two lunatics who had been firing in all directions. He knew it was a mistake to rely on this bunch of losers to transport and deliver the arsenal required to arm the terrorist cells that he had cultivated up and down the Country. It had taken the last eight years of his life to build the network.

He had worked tirelessly to set it up. His triumph had been only days away. He had stayed below the radar of the security services for all those years, slowly and meticulously recruiting. The amount of funding that was required had been immense. The money had been found no matter the cost. Now it was all disintegrating before him.

It had been total dedication, commitment and self sacrifice that had brought the plot this far. Every last penny had been spent to reach this moment. Now it was over.

He had been forced to use these idiots by his contacts in France. It was the only part of the operation he had no control over. The suppliers of the arms would only deal with their tried and trusted associates. The wanted no direct dealings with fanatics. They were businessmen and they knew that ideology and profits were not ideal bedfellows.

Mo had to use the middle men in France to get his shipment to the UK. He had no way of knowing that their tried and trusted routes across the Channel had been wiped out only a week before by a joint British and French secret service operation. He had no way of knowing that they had been separate from money and were short on contacts.

In a desperate bid to re-establish their fortune the arms smugglers in France had turned to the hapless bunch of small time drug and people smugglers that were Charlie, Neil and Bobby.

Mo had not planned it this way. He had rigged the van in which he had come to collect the arms with high explosives. He had decided a long time ago that he would not just be arrested quietly. He would take as many of the bastards with him as he could.

The van was behind him still a parked outside the lock up. There was confusion as Neil and Bobby died in the hail of police gun fire. On the ground beside him Charlie laid stock still. One policeman stood guard over them, distracted by the mayhem.

In Mo's mind this was the final reckoning. He had lost it all. He had been denied his revenge. He inched the mobile phone from pocket. The number was on speed dial. Two clicks of the finger were all that was required. When the call connected the bomb in the van would detonate. He would die and so would many others this night.

He glanced at his guard. He was not focussed on him, his attention elsewhere. He pressed the key pad on the phone. He waited for the sound of the phone connecting. He prayed to Allah. It rang. The explosion was much larger than he could have hope for. The policeman standing over him was tossed a side by the blast wave.

The police were decimated, killed, injured, maimed and

disorientated by the scale of the blast. He watched as it unfolded as if in a slow motion scene in an action film. Then it dawned on him. He was alive. He struggled to his feet. He was alive and unharmed apart from being rendered deaf by the blast wave.

He ran from the scene. Nobody followed. It was a miracle. God was indeed protecting him in his mission. He disappeared into the night unobserved by the convoy of police cars, ambulances and fire engines roaring past him to the site of the carnage he had caused.

Alone he took out his phone and sent an email telling of the disaster. The response was not long in coming. He smiled as he read it. He had a name. He had a hope. He had a mission again. He had a target. This time he must not fail. He had waited so long for this moment.

He smashed the phone and walked off into the night.

Chapter 20

"I don't think I am fully fit yet," said Tim.

"You seem to have recovered most of your mobility." Madeleine and Tim were in his old office in Thames House.

"Still have a weakness and they are not clear as to if I will ever regain full fitness but you are right the physiotherapy is working."

"The Home Office is looking for a permanent solution. They will not let me sit here for ever. They want a permanent replacement for you. Let's be honest they aren't going to give me the job."

"I can't see why not," said Tim.

"It's nice of you to say, being the token, black lesbian is one thing but actually holding power is another."

"I don't believe that and neither should you," said Tim. "You are really good at this job, better than me if the truth be told," said Tim.

"Well I agree with the latter part of that statement," she smiled. "But there are still a whole heap of arsehole bigots out there. I should know I have been black all my life. I may not be stopped and searched by the police every two minutes but the underlying attitude is still there."

"Well you were the police so you would be searching yourself."

"Right, but trust me, the prejudice is still there."

"To be honest I am surprised there hasn't been a move to oust me anyway. I am not the politician's favourite spy."

"They only have one thing on their mind and that is leaving the European Union, Brexit. They keep resigning from their ministerial posts over it. They don't stay in situ long enough to have a shake-up here," said Madeleine.

"How are we getting on with cooperation plans with the other European Agencies post Brexit, anyway?"

"We have plans for continuing intelligence sharing and enforcement but who knows what will happen."

"I do really think you are better suited to all this than me," said Tim.

"Boring, methodical and a lover of paperwork you mean?"

Tim said nothing and raised an eyebrow.

"Piss off," said Madeleine laughing.

"Anyway as I am here I think we ought to put our heads together on what just happened don't you?"

"I think it can more or less go down as a success, arms smugglers caught or killed, arms seized, nine terrorist cells closed down and all the terrorists in custody. MI5 can take the credit for stopping the biggest threat since the London bombings."

"Except..."

"Well except there are the dead and injured officers, the fact that the lead suspect escaped and we do not know what group or who was funding it."

"And there dear Madeleine is the problem. The people behind it are still out there and for all we know still have the money to get up and running immediately."

Madeleine picked up the phone. There was a short wait before

Harriet entered the office. "I was waiting for the call," she said as she came in carrying her iPad.

"Well?" said Madeleine.

"We have been interviewing the terrorists that were rounded up. No one knows who their contact was. This chap we call Mo seems to have no real history. Whereas most of the members of the cells up and down the Country seem to have grown up together, met training in Pakistan or Syria or were drawn together online. Our guy remains a mystery. It is like he was always there but nobody actually has any history with him. He seems to have just appeared eight or nine years ago."

"Do we have nothing on the chap?" said Tim.

"He has just come from nowhere," said Harriet. "He doesn't seem to fit any profiles on the database. We are trolling everything, so are the other Agencies and GCHQ. He is proving really hard to pin down but we will narrow in on him eventually. Everyone leaves a trail or makes a mistake. It is just a matter of time."

"Any luck with the funding?" said Madeleine.

"That is yielding some results but making sense of it is another matter."

"Well tell us what you have?" said Tim.

"Okay, the first thing is the amount. It is a lot. So the first thoughts were the Saudis. They have deep pockets and history."

"And?" said Madeleine.

"Not on the face of it, although they do not fund terrorism directly so making it harder to link it back to them but they do through various charities and agencies. It makes deniability easier."

"So where did this Mo get the money to fund the arms and operatives?"

"Next stop Pakistan," said Harriet. "The USA has been banging the international table about the Government saying one thing about fighting terrorism and on doing nothing to combat it. Given that a great number of those rounded up were of Pakistani descent it is an obvious place to look."

"So did the money come from some group in Pakistan?"

"Life is not that simple. You don't just write a cheque and make it payable to Mr Terrorist. The funding is passed through dummy accounts at a number of banks in Countries that have secrecy laws aimed at hiding rich tax dodgers. Unfortunately they also protect terrorists to the same extent."

"So no progress?" said Tim.

"Of course progress. I wouldn't waste your time if I didn't have something. It is just I can't make sense of it or tie it together."

"Stop telling what you don't know and tell us what you do know," said an irritated Madeleine.

Tim said nothing. Madeleine's style was a bit more direct than his. "Carry on," he urged.

Harriet gave Madeleine a glare and took a deep breath. "Thailand," she said.

"That's ridiculous," said Madeleine.

"Let's just hear it out," said Tim in an attempt to deescalate the tension brewing.

"As I said, I haven't figured it out yet. This has come from Customs and Excise not from the usual security sources. They picked up on large sums just being paid from a Bangkok bank to the UK. They were looking for money going out obviously to pay for drugs being imported into the UK but you get debits as well as credits. Some one at HMCR picked up on it and wondered what the Thais were buying from us."

"Well what were they spending their money on in the UK, real estate or football league clubs? That seems the preferred route for all the dodgy money flowing into the Country from tax dodging oligarchs and criminals around the Globe? London is the preferred money laundering destination of choice," said Tim.

"That's the point. They are buying nothing. They are paying dummy companies on fake invoices and getting nothing in return. The money vanishes."

"Vanishes?"

"Vanishes up until now," said Harriet. "Now we have turned our resources to, it seems that the money is then going to Eastern Europe, Albania. HMRC thought it was a valued added tax fraud. We know better. Some one, our Mo and his merry band of Jihadis is buying arms with the money."

"And where is the money coming from?" said Tim.

"From what appears to be an almost bankrupt agro-industrial group in Thailand called the Dawar Corporation."

Chapter 21

Tim felt exhausted and dehydrated. His head was pounding and his ears were still blocked from the change in pressure from the plane's descent. He knew that he was gradually recovering from the damage done to his brain but he tired easily especially when walking. He had never considered himself a dramatic person and was not prone to over reaction. He had discovered that this was only partly true.

He had fallen asleep on the long flight to Thailand and had the nightmare again. Over and over he would enter the barn. He would see Harriet tied and naked with her killer ready to strike, then black. The dream would rerun as on a loop. He would try and change the outcome but to no avail. There was always the black and pain.

He shook his head and held his nose. He blew down it and felt his ears pop. He could hear a bit better and the pain eased slightly below his ears as the pressure equalised.

He thought back over the last thirty hours. It had been difficult with Harriet. They had avoided the conversation during Tim's recover in hospital and then therapy. Something needed to be said but neither knew how to say it.

They had left Thames House and walked. They ended up sat on a bench on the Embankment. There was a long silence as they both stared out over the river. How many lovers had sat on this very spot over the years? How many hearts had been broken? How many hearts had been filled with hope and joy?

They sat in silence for a long while. The barges, passenger boats and all manner of water craft plied their business on the river. It was a distraction that they gratefully indulged. In the end one would have to speak. "We need to talk." It was Harriet.

"I know but I do not know what to say."

"Say you love me?" It was more a question than a command. She took his hand but could not hold his gaze. She was unsure. She felt exposed and vulnerable. There had been moments when she had been absolutely certain of his feelings for her, those moments that all lovers knew. The moment when a storm of emotion rushes over you, you know that it is just so right and the connection is total.

Tim looked ahead. He knew that she wanted his answer. He knew in his heart that he wanted her, to release himself into her love but. There was always the, but, the doubt and a sense he was betraying something fundamental to his being.

He had loved before. He had married Jackie. He had brought her into his world. In truth he had only been starting out in that world which now he realised was never what it seemed. A world where deceit was the reality and truth an illusion created by those in power. A world where there was no good or bad, just convenience masquerading as righteousness.

Jackie had died as had his best friend, Styles. He had continued to live and watched more people die. Harriet had nearly died. What of the next time? Would she join the list of people whom he had seen die?

He knew he should walk away from MI5. That was the right choice. Walk away and settle down. He knew that all he had to say were three short words. He knew she was waiting on him. He could feel the tension in her as she sat gazing at the Thames.

Slowly he turned to her. "I do love you but..."

The landing was bumpy and brought Tim back into the here and now. He was sad and filled with self doubt. Ultimately he had not committed to Harriet. She had walked away. He had not seen her tears but he felt her pain at rejection and his own guilt. He had never really had a choice. He knew that what he felt at that moment, sitting by the river that he was not destined for a normal life. He had learned that lesson and he would heed it.

It was selfish act. It was however inevitable. The deaths of his wife and colleagues weighed heavy. It was a debt he owed, a debt that had been run up in blood. He could not walk away. He felt it was his duty to continue to fight and defend those that depended on him and his ilk, for their safety and security. On a basic level it was guilt that drove him on and it provided justification for his self denial of happiness.

Tim felt, as he watched Harriet walk away along the crowded pavement of the Embankment, that he was freeing her. He felt he was protecting her, removing her from danger. The decision that he was going to go back and take up his job as Director of MI5 had been made in those few moments sitting on a bench with the woman he loved.

"I am going to Bangkok," Tim said.

"Are you sure?" He had returned to MI5 HQ and had made his way to Madeleine's office, his office.

"I need to do something and I am not ready for all the paperwork, endless meetings and the humouring of politicians yet."

"You are definitely coming back?" said Madeleine.

"I know you wanted the job..."

"I am disappointed but I am also realistic. The odds on my being appointed were very low and I know in my heart that you are the better candidate. So, don't feel too bad."

"That was a kind thing to say."

"And the truth and that is not a good trait to have in this job. Honesty and transparency is a real hindrance."

He laughed. "So book my ticket and let's see if we can't get to the bottom of all this."

Tim had the file on Dawar and he would be met by an attaché on arrival, Phillip Hetherington. Every Government's Embassies had their quota of spies attached. Attaché was shorthand for spy. They were on the host Countries list and would be the first to be expelled when and if there was a spat between the two Countries. Their duties were intelligence gathering and surface espionage. The real spying was far more clandestine and covert.

Tim was not here to spy and the Thai agencies were fully informed of his arrival. He hoped that he would be able to get things moving. His aim was to meet and put pressure on with the right people in the right positions. There was a real and imminent threat to the UK and he wanted it addressing. The key seemed to be a Thai Corporation, Dawar. Money spoke in Thailand and he needed to cut through the red tape and bribery and dig down into Dawar. His presence should focus minds.

"Will you take Harriet?" Madeleine had asked.

"No not this time," Tim had replied.

She said nothing and there was an awkward silence. She picked up a report and handed it to him. "This came to light when we ran the checks on Dawar."

"Who's Suzy Webb?"

"Ex-copper, she seems to have gone missing in Thailand. You know the Met they like to look after their own so they are casting wide and far to find her."

"You want me to ask around and see what I can find out?"

"Don forget I was technically a copper before I took the job here as deputy Director so I see no harm in helping my former colleagues. It cuts both ways we will need their help sooner or later. Anyway if you read on there is a link."

Tim looked back at the file. "Oh Dawar," he said.

"She went missing after visiting their HQ. She was assessing them for some sort of green energy grant for the Asian Green Energy development Agency, AGENDA. She seemed to vanish into thin air. "

Chapter 22

"I have been laying the ground work with the Thai Police or at least trying to," said Phillip Hetherington.

They were sat in Tim's hotel room. Phillip Hetherington was a studious looking you man in his early thirties, slightly balding with glasses. "What do you mean by trying?" asked Tim.

"To put it kindly they have their own way of going about things. Dawar is seen as a good employer and I suspect as a good source of bribes for the people who run things here. They have no need to start turning over stones and seeing what crawls out. Dawar has done nothing wrong here in Thailand and we have no proof they have done anything wrong in the UK. So what good reason would the authorities her have for upsetting the apple cart?"

"I see," said Tim. "What about this missing woman working for the energy agency, Agenda. She has gone missing here, in Thailand. That is on their soil. Are they investigating her disappearance? That gives us a way into Dawar surely?"

"I have pushed, trust me. They are in no hurry. As far as they are concerned, it is a missing person case. There is no evidence of foul play. Hundreds go missing every year. She is an adult and she has the right to do what she wants. It is not even an immigration issue. She has a valid visa." Phillip shrugged.

Tim was finding it hard to hide his frustration. He was tired from the journey and the last thing he wanted to hear was that he was going to get little or no help from the Thai agencies. He trusted Harriet's instincts. If she said that Dawar had funded the failed terrorist's attacks in the UK then they had. He was here to stop the source of funding and ensure that there would be no more attacks in the future.

"If they won't help we need to make something happen to force their hand. They key is this missing woman. He looked at the file. She had a meeting scheduled with Dawar, in Chiang Mai at their HQ, Did she go?"

"She went. A chap called Somchai Onruang set it up and she met with the head of the Company. They presented proposals for an energy programme and an outline agreement was reached for AGENDA support. That is what Dawar says anyway."

"She then disappears off the face of the planet?"

"Not quite, according to the police after her meeting she went out for a night on the town. She ended up at a night club, come knocking shop. They say she left and then doesn't return to the hotel," said Phillip.

Tim thought for a moment. How about we take the line that her meeting with Dawar didn't rum as smooth as they claim. Who knows perhaps she discovered some sort of financial irregularities in her due diligence work for AGENDA. They realise they could be in hot water and conveniently get rid of her."

"A bit far fetched," said Phillip.

"I did not say it was realistic merely a way to start digging."

"You need some form of proof to get them to open an investigation."

"Like this," said Tim? He handed a file across the table to him.

He sat and read. "Is this true?"

"No idea, I asked Harriet Shaw to put it together before I left. It looks convincing to me," he smiled.

It was suddenly dawning on Phillip just why Tim was Director

General and he was an attaché. The file was a masterpiece in its own way. It drew together fact and superstition and weaved it into a compelling indictment of Dawar as a money laundering and terrorist funding hub.

"As we speak, our Ambassador has an appointment with Government Officials here. He will be threatening exposing Thailand's lack of commitment to tacking global threats of terrorist activity. They will have to respond positively or risk looking bad on the international stage." Tim looked at his watch.

As if on cue his mobile phone rang. He conversation was brief, "I'll send my chap over right away, His name is Phillip Hetherington. Thank you for your cooperation."

Phillip looked at Tim. "Well off you go," said Tim

"Where?" said Phillip.

"Paruskavan Palace, Thai National Intelligence Agency, take the file. They are expecting you, "said Tim. "I am going to have a little sleep and I'll see you back here in a couple of hours."

It seemed to Tim that he had only been asleep for a matter of minutes when the phone beside his bed rang. It was Phillip and he was back from his visit with the Thai secret service. Phillip sat in the living room while Tim had a shower and dressed.

"Well how did it go?"

"You certainly put the cat among the pigeons," said Phillip.

"Go on."

"It was a smorgasbord of Thai uniforms that greeted me. I have never seen so many peaked caps and gold braid in one room in my life."

"So our little file and a bit of political pressure have forced the pace a bit?"

"Well more than a bit. The fixer for Dawar, Somchai Onruang is now on their radar. They are hunting for him. It seems that nothing goes on without somebody knowing something. After a bit of digging they have found a port official who now remembers that Dawar needed access to a shipment of Jade in transit to China."

"When you say remembers?"

"Not so much remembered as bribed to forget whatever shenanigans Somchai Onruang was up to at the docks. Threatened with a trip to a Thai prison, he and the port officials had a sudden clarity of recall."

"I see and what is the net result?"

"The Dawar Corporation is to be investigated for customs fraud. It is not sponsoring terrorism but it is a way for the Intelligence Service to start digging into them."

"Well that file worked better then I had expected," said Tim.

"What is our next move," asked Phillip.

"Well if I were Somchai Onruang I would really like to avoid being interrogated by the Thai secret service. They do not have a reputation for gentle dealings with detainees. I am guessing he has by now realised that he is between a rock and a hard place. On the one hand if he is interrogated and talks he will be a dead man. If on the other, he is now the target for the terrorists who will kill him too ensure he can't talk. Either way his future looks uncertain."

"Well let's hope the authorities catch up with him and offer him some sort of protection and immunity."

"Really," mused Tim. "I think that you may be being overly optimistic. Don't you feel that, given you knowledge of the level of corruption that everybody and his dog now knows that Somchai Onruang is now on the wanted list? Do you think that some unfortunate accident will before him before he can talk?"

"Phillip looked puzzled. "There is little we can do though. On your reasoning he will be killed either by Dawar, terrorists or accidentally in police custody."

"Let's hope he comes to the same conclusion."

"Why," said Phillip?

"Why? Because I am just about to become Mr Onruang's best friend, not only his best friend, but his only friend. We are going to save his arse and he is going to help us round up the bastards that want to blow up innocent people on the streets of Britain."

Chapter 23

The squat in Laindon in Essex, on the borders of London was inhabited by a small group of addicts. Mo had taken up a small room at the rear of the property. Here he was anonymous. The other inhabitants had no interest in their fellow house guests. Their only interest was in finding enough money to obtain their next fix.

Mo knew he was one of the most wanted men in the Country at the moment. The police would be chasing down every cell member across the Country, follow every lead and security would be on its highest alert. Years of planning had gone into what was to have been the biggest terror attack ever to be staged on British soil. He had devoted nearly nine years of his life to bringing it about. It had been taken from him at the last moment. He felt empty only his hatred fuelled him and propelled him on.

His phone call had given him hope. He knew that there was a backup plan to cause chaos and death. It would take time. He had waited so long and now just when the end had been in sight he was forced to be patient again.

The new plan was to be a statement, an all out attack at the heart of the British establishment. It would not be up close and personal though. It would not give him the satisfaction he craved. He wanted the, one on one, destruction of a single person. He wanted to see them die. He wanted to pull the trigger and watch them die.

A week at least was all he had to wait. He did not want to wait a week. He had a name now. The email had given the name of the person he wanted dead. For Mo that death was the only reason for his being. Yes there was a better plan, a more certain plan, a less risky plan to get revenge on all those that had wronged him and his family but it was not so intimate. He wanted to kill hands on.

Sitting on the dirty mattress in the drug house he knew he would not wait further. The longer he waited the more the chance of his being tracked down and arrested. There was one person he wanted dead above anything and he wanted it now.

He made his way into the damp street and walked to the café. He used the free Wi-F there, on the unregistered cell phone he had bought. He searched and found what he wanted. He could hardly believe it. It was as though God was on his side. He knew it was fate. It had just come together for him.

He phoned. "I have to do this," he said.

"No, please don't. What if you fail? All the planning all the effort and all the money will have been for nothing."

Mo was deaf to reason. His mind was set. Nothing could reason with him. He had waited so long to be avenged that it burned into his brain and he could not resist. He had his target and he would prevail. He believed. He boarded the train for the City. He had a busy twenty four hours ahead. Tomorrow was his moment then his target would be in the cross airs of his riffle. He knew he would be caught and most likely killed but it made it all the easier to kill. He did not need to plan for or have an escape.

Ibrahim put down the phone. He knew he had lost control. Mo was set on this suicide mission and was beyond reason. He understood why he would not wait but it was the wrong move. If Mo failed than the target would have been warned and then all his careful planning would be wasted, years of work all for nothing.

He knew that they were closing in on him. It was now a race. General Xi had been good to his word. The bargain had been kept and the package was in England. It was being assembled at this very moment. It would be ready to use within the week. Mo had only to wait a few days but that was not to happen. There was nothing to be done the die was cast.

His connections, the officials that took money from Dawar kept him informed. The arrival of Mr Burr from MI5 had changed everything. He had put pressure on and the Thai police and secret service could not afford to ignore Dewar's activities. It was only a matter of time before the edifice crumbled and he would be exposed.

The weak link was Somchai Onruang. He had always been the risk. He was only interested in money. His loyalty only went as deep as the pockets paying him. Ibrahim had needed him. As a Pakistani, Muslim, a foreigner it would have been impossible to carry out his designs here in Thailand.

Dawar had needed his contacts above all. Somchai could ease Ibrahim and Dawar's activities. He was the grease that lubricated the machinery of corruption that had allowed him to do business under the radar. Dawar had done the deal for the Jade with Xi but only Somchai could actually get it from Myanmar to China. Only he had the contacts. He had served his purpose and now he was a threat.

Somchai Onruang had gone to ground. He knew that the Secret Service were after him. He knew that Dawar would want him silenced and he was certain the General Xi would not want their dealings being made known to the Chinese. He had few friends left but bribing officials in the police kept him in the loop.

MI5 and the Thai Intelligence were another matter. They could not be bribed to look the other way while he quietly left the Country and took up a new identity abroad. He had laid plans for a sudden departure years before. His plans had however focussed on avoiding taxation authorities and emigration. The bombing in London and raised the anti. He was wanted in connection with international terrorism not just a bit of dodgy business dealing.

Somchai Onruang knew he was busted. It was just a coin flip as to who got to him first. When he had joined with Dawar he thought it was just another business scam. Getting the jade out and making loads of money seemed a good idea and he liked making loads of money. If

General XI and his cronies were lining their pockets it was no concern of his that they were cutting out their bosses in mainland China. It was also not of interest if Ibrahim made a fortune moving the Jade.

The bit of the puzzle that now saw him in this position was that Dawar was using its money to fund Jihadis in Britain. Now Ibrahim needed him gone and the General Xi needed him gone. He was the common link to the Jade, the Chinese and terrorist funding from Dawar.

He sat contemplating his position. He knew there were few options on the table and none good. He picked up his cell phone and dialled the number.

"British Consular Service" was the response.

"May I speak to the Consular Attaché please?" His call was put through.

The Thai operator listened to the exchange for a few moments. "I need a cigarette break," he said handing over his switchboard duties to a colleague.

He made his way outside and lit his cigarette. He keyed in the number he had written on the flap of the cigarette flap. He waited and until the call was answered. "I have what you want."

He followed the directions he had been given over the phone. He soon found the rubbish bin. There was a plastic carrier bag placed there moments before his arrival. He removed it and checked the contents. He knew that he was being watched. The money was in the bag. Satisfied he threw the cigarette packet into the bin and made his way back to work.

The packet was immediately retrieved from the bin by the watcher. He lifted the flap and there was written the address. He pulled his phone from his pocket and spoke to the voice on the other end. "He has arranged a meeting with the British." He gave the time and place.

Chapter 24

"We have him," said Phillip as he rushed into his office which Tim had taken over.

"Somchai Onruang?" said Tim.

"Yes, I have spoken to him. He wants to do a deal."

"What sort of deal?" said Tim.

"He gives us all we need on Dawar and in return we get him out and a new life."

"Not much choice is there. We need to know what the threat is and stop it. It is always the same we have to deal with people like him to stop worse people. Where is he?"

Phillip Hetherington handed Tim a piece of paper. "He will meet us here."

"Stupid of me to ask really, it means nothing," said Tim.

Phillip laughed." Shall we take a cab then?"

The Bangkok traffic was horrendous as always. The taxi smelt of garlic and cigarettes. The driver was taking constantly trying to drum up business, either driving them where they did not want to go or taking them to a guide he knew, who would show them sights they did not want to see.

"Just drive us where we want to go," said Phillip in Thai.

The driver shut up. "Are you a linguist?"

"Not really but I did a gap year that turned into a bit longer. I picked it up then. I volunteered to come back when the posting came up," said Phillip.

"Could be worse," said Tim.

"It is okay. I thought I was in love and wanted to get back here."

"Happy ever after?" said Tim.

"I was young and a naïve."

"Well you are still young."

"And now I am cynical."

Tim laughed," Well that's the main qualification in this job."

The cab pulled up. Tim let the attaché pay as he looked around him. This was along way from the main tourist strip. There were small business, roller doors and factory units.

"Where is it?"

Phillip looked up and down the street. "I am not sure." He pulled his cell phone from his pocket and checked the sat nav. "The bastard has dropped us about two blocks away."

"Let's get walking then."

Somchai Onruang was looking at his watch. He had decided that he would be safer in the anonymous office building than walking up the street to the British Embassy. He suspected that the Embassy here and the Consulate in Chiang Mai would be now watched. By making contact with MI5 he hoped that they would organise protection for him. They were late. He was becoming agitated.

He walked to the window and looked down onto the street again. There was nothing. He knew the longer he was on the streets the more at risk he was. He did not know fully know what Ibrahim was involved in but he knew too much. He was not blind. He knew about the disappearance of Suzy Webb. He knew about the Jade and he knew about the Chinese.

It did not know what was delaying the British. He was pacing back and forth as the seconds ticked by. He stopped as the door opened. He had not heard anyone approach over the sound of his own footsteps.

"At last," he said.

It was the last words he uttered. There was a loud bang and the bullet entered his chest. He felt no pain just a sensation like he had been pushed hard. The bullet had missed his heart but he was struggling to breath where it had punted his lung.

He sank to his knees and lent forward supporting himself on his left arm. He saw the shoes of his assailant as he walked across the room to where he knelt, head down and gasping for air. The feet stopped in front of him.

There was another loud bang as his killer fired the second fatal shot into the top of his bowed head. Life gone his body toppled forward. The shooter used his foot to roll the body sideways onto his back.

He bent over Somchai and avoiding the blood and brain tissue and carefully searched the pockets. Satisfied he had everything he checked the room closing the door behind him.

When he reached the street he realised that the shots had been heard. He had to hurry from the scene. He did not want to be there when the police arrived. He hastily walked a few streets away before finding a taxi. He pulled his phone from his pocket,

It was answered immediately by Ibrahim. They spoke in Arabic. "It is done."

"Peace be upon you," was the response.

"What the hell is going on?" said Tim. He was breathless from the walk. The weakness left over from his injury still made it difficult for him. He was getting stronger but he realised he still had a way to go before he was his old self.

The road was cordoned off with police tape. The police cars with their light still flashing had blocked the road ahead. An ambulance was parked at the scene. It was clear that there was no urgency in the crew's movements. There was no reason for speed they were dealing with a dead body.

Tim approached the tape and was stopped by a uniformed policeman. He showed him id and asked to speak to the officer in charge. After a twenty minute wait a young man approached him. It turned out his English was limited and Tim was forced to wait while Phillip engaged the detective. Eventually the detective walked off and Phillip turned his attention to Tim.

"Someone's been shot, a Thai in his mid forties. It was a professional job, finished off with a close up head shot. It seems to be Somchai. It is at the address we were going to and the description matches the photo we have on file for him," said Phillip.

"It would appear that someone has beaten us to him. That makes it all a bit more difficult," said Tim.

"Phillip was a bit shocked at Tim's mater of fact assessment. "Someone had been murdered," he said.

Tim looked at him. "Someone, who had little to no concern for anyone, someone who was quite happy to see dead innocent, men, women and children on Britain's streets as long as he profited by it. I think you sympathy would be better spent on the real victims. Don't you?"

He realised that there was a reason why the man before him was in the job he was. He was a realist but he cared. He cared for his Country and the people that lived there. He would always do what was necessary, whatever the cost to himself and others to protect it. In his own way he was a fanatical as any Islamic extremist in his determination to win. In his own quite unassuming way he was deadly.

"Sorry," said Phillip.

"Don't be silly. Death is never good. I don't want anyone to die or suffer but we are here to defend the decent everyday people trying to get on with their lives. Sometimes to do that we have to be prepared to accept the realities of life," he paused.

"Now go and find us a cab. I am feeling the effects of walking. I am still not fully recovered yet."

He watched as Phillip walked up the street to get a taxi. The area was chaos with the Police still blocking both ends of the road. Tim was watched as Phillip rounded the corner. His leg was beginning to drag and he limped slowly after him. He paused to catch his breath and rest his leg.

He was distracted and off guard, not paying attention to his surroundings. The hood was over his head and all went black before he knew what was happening. The two men pulled him across the pavement into the van before he had a chance to react. Tim had been abducted and was a block away before Phillip returned looking for him.

Chapter 25

Gerald Inglewood sat in the office waiting for the last customer of the day. He had three bookings that day for trips in the vintage planes and a regular taking flying lessons for a private pilot's license. The De Havilland Tiger Moth was out of action so he had taken them up in the Piper L18C Super Cub. It was not as iconic as the Tiger Moth but it still gave the old school flying experience.

Winter was approaching and bookings were drying up. In truth it was more a labour of love than a business. Gerald loved to fly and the trips in the old planes just about funded his hobby. He knew he could not continue much longer. The cost of the hanger, repairs, fees and fuel just kept rising.

The two Pakistanis who had booked in for the vintage flight experienced had come via an online voucher scheme. It allowed you to buy a gift voucher and then phone one of several providers nationwide to book a lesson. The voucher scheme had not been a great success. He had three of four bookings as a result but after commission was deducted he barley made a profit from it.

They were well spoken and well dressed. "We are not interested in learning to land," the first had said.

Gerald's face had been a picture. It conjured up the terrible events of 9/11 when terrorist had crashed two passenger jets into the twin Trade Towers in New York. They had gained access to the flight deck and taken control. It emerged after that some of them had taken flying lessons in Florida but had shown no interest in the landing procedure.

The second laughed uproariously at the expression on Gerald's face. "We are joking," he said.

Inglewood Flying Company was based at Shoreham south of the Capital. It consisted of a rented hanger with an office, three planes, two vintage and one old, a few desks, computer and a phones. Outside there was a few picnic tables where friends and spectators could sit and watch. Its bank account was overdrawn.

The conversation had developed. It was clear to Gerald that the two young men shared his interest in aviation. In fact they seemed very knowledgeable in deed. In fact had he really thought about it they were far too knowledgeable for a couple of City boys thinking of taking up flying as a hobby? He did not think about it though.

The story they seemed entirely plausible. It ran along the lines of they and a group of their friends, traders, brokers and finance people who all worked together in the City had been toying with setting up a flying club. "More money than sense," had been Gerald's first thought. He had encouraged them. After all he was virtually bankrupt so he was not about to look a gift horse in the mouth.

His last ever customer turned upon on time. He spent an hour going through the theory before he took to the air. His solo flight was successful. The planes were back in the hanger and the new happy pilot had left. Gerald was feeling nostalgic. He would miss all this. It had been part of his life for so long. He knew that he had to move on. He was not getting any younger and at least this way he would have some money in the bank.

His phone alerted him to a text. He opened the message. "Congratulations check you bank account." He waited while the six year old Acer laptop powered up. It took him a while to log onto his bank account. He was most shocked to see the large positive balance he was so used to it being an overdraft.

Gerald Inglewood was no longer the owner of Inglewood Aviation. A company registered in Gibraltar was its new owner. All that was left was to hand over the keys to the new owners.

He had emailed and written to his clients and business connections to say he was retiring and that Inglewood Aviation would be closed for a few months for refurbishment.

He checked round the office and packed his few remaining personal possessions in a cardboard box and carried them out to his car. As he climbed the external steps that led back to the office, above the hanger the two men arrived. He waited for them as the approached.

The two men entered the office behind him. "I have left the books and keys on the desk," he was saying as he walked over to the coat rack to retrieve his overcoat. He never finished the sentence.

The bullet fired from the silenced gun hit him in the back of the head. By signing the sale of the Company he had signed his own death warrant. The body was carried from the office down the flight of internal steps into the hanger. It would be left there to be discovered by the police at some stage.

The two men returned to the office and began stripping it bare. "We need to get all this stuff removed and dumped. It is barely large enough as it is without all this junk it."

They worked round the clock and piled everything in the seating area. It was a small grass covered patch surrounded by a low wooden fence. There were two oblong picnic tables and four benches where the friends and relatives could sit while a flight in a vintage plane was in progress. This area was now the rubbish tip.

They had barely finished dumping everything in the garden when the rubbish collection truck turned up. The driver and his mate began loading and after two hours the contents of the office was on the loader and being driven off.

While the rubbish was leaving, two electricians arrived and began rewiring. The old wiring was ripped out. New wiring was installed. The electricians had been supplied with detailed drawings and specifications. "Blimey mate, what are you doing here, sending a rocket to the moon," one had asked?

"It's aviation you can't have dodgy wiring, health and safety," had been the reply.

It had taken four days of blood, Gerald's blood, sweat and tears the new owner's sweat and the control room was ready. The monitors, radar feeds and state of the art guidance and positioning equipment was in place and tested.

"All systems are go," joked one of the pilots.

Pilot was the correct word. The two were both ex military pilots. They had found it hard to feign ineptitude while they ingratiate themselves in to Gerald's good graces and earned his trust. It had been no accident that they had selected that small failing flying school. A lot of research and planning had gone into targeting him.

Inglewood Aviation had everything they were looking for. The hanger was on the extreme edge of the airfield away from view. The airfield was a short flying distance to London. Above all Gerald Inglewood was an eccentric with no family and was not going to be missed in the short term.

The next few days were tense for the two men. The delivery was fraught with risk. The package was being air freighted. That meant it had to get through customs. Shipping would have decreased the risk but the time scale was not acceptable. Speed was critical but it increased the risk of the cargo being flagged and intercepted. The likelihood of a physical inspection at the container ports was remote. The volume was far too high, the manifest and paperwork was the only viable method of tracking illicit traffic. The rate of inspection of air cargo was slightly higher but still only around five or six per cent for actually physical inspections.

They need not have worried the cargo passed through without incidence. The articulated truck pulled up only hours after the plane had landed. The three planes that had occupied the hanger had been pushed onto the hard standing to the front. The new arrival was easy to manoeuvre into the now vacant space.

"We've done it," said the first pilot.

"Now we begin checking, testing and double testing."

"Then we will teach them a lesson that will go down in history."

"Allah is great, praise be to Him."

Chapter 26

Tim was taken firmly in the grip of two men who guided him along a corridor and up some steps. He still had the dense black hood over his head. He was confused and his leg ached terribly from being forced to crouch in the rear of the van. One minute he had been standing in the street waiting for Phillip to return with a taxi, the next he had been bundled into the back of a vehicle and was being bounced back and forth as the driver avoided the heavy traffic.

No one had spoken and he had no idea who had abducted him or where he was being taken. He knew he had been taken from the van and walked to an elevator. He assumed that he had arrived in an underground car park and his captors had transported him via the lift into the building.

Neither his hands nor feet had been bound. He sat. He could feel the presence of two men. One sat either side of him. They each rested a hand on his wrist letting it be known that should he try to escape that they would be quite capable of restraining him. Tim for his part had no intention of engaging his captors in a physical confrontation. For one he was hooded and could see nothing and in any event he doubted he would get the better of then and make good any form of escape.

He sat quietly. Suddenly the hood was pulled from his head. He was blinded by the light as his eyes tried to adjust from total darkness. There was a flash. He assumed it was the flash of a camera phone and that he had been photographed. The hood was then replaced as quickly as it had been removed.

The whole episode had been so brief that he had no time to see anything clearly. He had caught the merest glimpse of the camera and the shadowy figure holding it before the hood was replaced. The flash of light had left him seeing a kaleidoscope of flashing light dots as though he had walked from bright sunlight into a darkened room.

Tim was not quite sure as to how long he had been seated between his two new close companions but time moved slowly. He was anxious. The increased flow of adrenaline, occasioned by the situation, caused more alertness in him but also seemed to slow time down. Perhaps he had been there ten minutes or perhaps he had sat for an hour. He was unsure but the longer he sat waiting the greater the tension in him.

Without warning he was pulled to his feet. There had been no words spoken so he assumed that they had been summoned to move by a gesture alone. As he was guided forward he became away that the floor had changed from stone of tile to deep plush carpet beneath his feet. There was the sound of opening door before he was taken further into a room and sat in a very comfortable arm chair.

The hood was removed and he blinked at the sudden brightness. As he eyes adjusted Tim's first thoughts were that he was in a very expensive and ornately decorated Chinese restaurant. Two men were leaving and had their backs to him. These were presumably the men who had held him prisoner. As they departed he realised that he was not in a restaurant but some sort of ornately decorated dinning room. It was however stuffed with Chinese artefacts and decorated in red and gold.

"Welcome to the Chinese Embassy, my name is David Chan," a smartly dressed man of Chinese ethnicity introduced himself as though this was a normal first meeting. He walked over and offered Tim his hand. Tim still slight disorientated by his recent experiences took it and shook it without thinking.

"Well you must qualify as one of the World's most polite kidnappers." There was a certain amount of sarcasm in Tim's voice as he shook the proffered hand.

David Chan laughed. "I am really sorry. It was a bit of a cock up I am afraid." It was clear from his accent that David had received at some stage the best education the British could offer. Tim could spot Eton and Oxford from the first spoken vowel in a sentence.

Tim was not in the mood to take the matter with humour. Abducting the head of another Country's Security service was not something that should be indulged in lightly. They were both aware that it was just not done. Well not unless you wanted to provoke an international incident or possibly a war.

"What in the hell are you doing. Do you know who I am?" Tim said realising that he sounded a bit like some film star pulled over by a local cop for speeding. "That didn't come out quite right but you know what I mean. We have an unwritten agreement nobody harms each others security chiefs. It would be bloody chaos. Can I leave or do you intend to keep me prisoner"

David looked slight abashed. "I did say I was sorry old boy. It was an accident..."

"What sort of accident involves pulling up in the street, popping a hood over somebody's head and dragging them into a van and driving off?"

"The sort of accident that happens when the head of MI5 turns up at a murder scene when no one knows he is in Thailand?" said David in a slightly questioning voice.

Tim could not help a little smile. "Go on tell me about how this accident happened?"

"Perhaps we could discuss it over dinner. We have one of the best Cantonese chiefs in the World her at the Embassy." He pointed to the table at the far end of the room, laid for two.

Tim gave the matter some thought. Whilst he wanted to preserve his dignity and insist on his immediately release to lodge a formal protest, he balanced the fact that he was hungry and the food sounded like it was to be spectacular. Appetite conquered indignity. "Do I have your word that I am free to leave at any time?"

"Of course we will provide a limo to take you back. I assure you that it was a complete mix up and it would honour me greatly if we could overlook the incident. Treat it as an invitation to dinner albeit slightly forceful."

"Well if you insist," he said as he sat down at the table.

David Chan had not lied as to the quality of the food. Course after course came up all equally delicious. Finally they settled back with a glass of port each before them. "Cigar?" said David.

"No thank you, I am fine," said Tim. "Now tell me what is going on?"

David paused briefly and Tim could see that the matter was of some delicacy. The next sentence confirmed this. "We find ourselves in a very difficult position and I need you to treat this with a certain amount of discretion, obviously only to the extent that you can within the bounds of what is in your Countries National interest. What lee way you can offer in the matter would be greatly appreciated. We do not want to turn a bad situation into an even worse incident if it can be avoided."

"Okay I'll do what I can. I have no wish to escalate the situation with China. So start with why you kidnapped me," said Tim.

"We have had a piece of valuable and highly potent bit of military hardware go missing. We are not sure where it has ended up at this precise moment. We have however tracked the involvement of a Thai National in the theft. A chap called Somchai Onruang."

"That is interesting," observed Tim.

"You know him then. It was our intention to pick him up and ask him for the name of the person who he was dealing with in China and why."

"But when you located him he was dead."

"Exactly then my agents saw you asking about him and made a spur of the moment decision to grab you and find out what your involvement was. They did not know who you were of course or they would not have done it."

"Ah the photo you took."

"Yes we ran it through the data base and we had a bit of a shock when we found we had..."

"Accidentally kidnapped the Director General of Mi5," said Tim.

"Could happen to anyone," David smiled lamely.

"Okay as I get it. Someone in your military has nicked a bomb or something and to find out who, you wanted to ask Somchai Onruang?"

"In a nutshell," said David.

"I was there to offer him asylum and in return he was going to reveal details of funding and the terrorists, active in the UK. It looks like we were both beaten to the punch."

"But who by?"

"With that I may be able to help you. We have traced his employer through following the money trail."

"Are you going to tell me?"

"That my friendly kidnapper depends on how forthright you are with me and if I believe what you tell me."

David Chan thought briefly. He had few options and working with MI5, the only one on the table. "Alright it is very Chinese though. We have a national passion for Jade. It is prized above gold and even diamonds, pure white is the most desired. Of course between us those that control its import are rich and influential."

"Go on," said Tim.

"The best Jade comes from Myanmar across the Chinese border.

The military in both countries have the trade sewn up between them. How ever a vast quantity of top quality stone had entered the country from another source. This has upset the wealthy elite that control the trade that lines their pockets."

"And they want the new kid on the block caught and eliminated?" said Tim.

"Yes but that was not really my problem. It became my problem when we lost a bit of military equipment. Who ever imported the Jade seems to have done a deal to supply said bit of kit as payment."

"Somchai Onruang was your only link to the Jade and your lost hardware?"

"And he is now dead. I need to recover or destroy the hardware and the only way of doing so is tracking the person who imported the jade and organised the swap. It has to be someone high up in China's military. That of course makes him very dangerous." said David.

Tim made a decision and spoke. "I can tell you who Somchai Onruang was working for but the same person is possibly in the process of funding the biggest terrorist attack targeting the UK. We need to nullify the threat. If I give that name we will have lost out only link to stopping the attack."

What do you want from us in return?"

"It is pretty cleat to me that not only is this individual putting up the cash for the Jihadis in the UK but he is planning on deploying this missing weapon of yours against us on British soil."

"Give me the name. We will get the get everything we need from him. The name of the person who imported the Jade stole the hardware and the details of any attack on the UK for you and everyone involved."

"The lost weapon..?"

"Trust me we will extract what we need from anyone we take into custody. It may take months for you to work with the Thai authorities to make progress. You may not ever get to speak to your suspect. Give me his name and I guarantee you will get what you need in hours."

Tim knew that he was effectively consenting to the abduction and torture of Ibrahim the head of Dawar industries. He knew that they had lost the chance of a quick resolution with the death of Somchai Onruang. While MI5 would be trying to even speak to Ibrahim the UK would be facing the possibility of innocent people maimed and dead on the streets. He made his decision.

"Where have you been?" said Philip.

"Dinner at the Chinese Embassy," said Tim. "Now book me a flight home."

"What about Ibrahim?"

"Oh I think you will find that he has already gone missing. I doubt he will be found by us or the Thai Police."

Chapter 27

Madeleine Wilson was sitting at her desk reading the communiqué from the Home Secretary. Madeleine had not even had a chance to meet her. The arguments over Britain's leaving the European Union meant that ministers left and joined the cabinet more frequently than most people had a hot bath. The previous incumbent had resigned only the week before.

The head of MI6 had been on television upping threat levels after the arrests of the terrorists. Without actually saying so he had claimed the round up of the terror cells established by Mo as an MI6 success. He had failed to mention that Mo had not been caught. This left the Home Office with MI5 looking incompetent.

The letter from the Home Secretary to Madeleine was almost a direct instruction for her to meet the press and bang the drum for MI5. She wanted in made clear that they had been responsible for stopping the threat and take the credit. The escape of Mo and the botched round up at the warehouse was somehow to be glossed over without blaming the Police's Counter Terrorist Unit. As a parting shot the Home Secretary had made it clear that she expected Mo, as he had been named, to be caught within say 48 hours.

Madeleine reread the letter and exhaled loudly. "Bollocks," she said.

Harriet looked up. She had remained behind after the meeting with the other departmental directors to discuss the latest Russian cyber intelligence reports. This was again linked to the new Home Secretary who as a fervent supporter of remaining in the European Union was looking for evidence of Russian interference in the Referendum which led to the people's decision to leave. She wanted to discredit the original plebiscite and so justify a second referendum. Harriet knew the Russians had manipulated social media as they had done prior to the US Presidential election but the Home Secretary was looking for something more meaty and substantial to raise a direct link.

"I think that is bit of a harsh indictment. We can now directly link thousands of bot accounts to the GRU, the Russian Secret Service. These automated, "bots" created a whole groundswell of anti EU propaganda …"

"Not bollocks to that, bollocks to my having to do a PR job for the Home Secretary," said Madeleine.

"Oh," said Harriet having no idea what the acting head of MI5 was taking about.

"I have to contrive to appear in public and get media coverage. I am requested to quote "reassure the public and inform them of MI5's recent success in counter terrorism." How am I supposed to do that? We know for a fact that the ring leader has escaped and is still out there with a shit load of cash supplied by this Dawar Corporation. "

"Well it was a success," said Harriet.

"Yes to the point the Mo turns up with another cell or two that we know nothing of as yet and blows up Westminster."

"Well it may be a technical failure if he blows up Parliament but on the positive side it would give the rest of us a break from the constant bickering about Brexit," joked Harriet.

"Not funny," said Madeleine. "We would look like a bunch of nincompoops if this Mo was behind another terror attack. I would be on record as blowing our own trumpet as to how successful we had been and then having to explain why there was carnage on the Country's streets."

"Refuse," said Harriet.

"I want to but that would not get us off to a great start with the new Home Secretary."

"Well you are in charge. She can't order you."

"Possibly not but it is budget time and then the Government Spending Review. It is not a bad thing to have the Minister on your side when you go to the Treasury asking for money though."

Madeleine sat looking at the letter, mumbling. Finally she said "bollocks" as she pushed it to one side. Just as she spoke the door opened,

"Well that's a nice way to greet me," said Tim as he entered her office.

"I thought you were in Bangkok?"

"Sorted that and came home," he said removing his top coat and throwing it over a vacant chair, He crossed the room and sat along side Harriet opposite Madeleine.

Madeleine cocked her head enquiringly.

Tim smiled and said nothing. "Shall I leave?" said Harriet.

"No you don't want to miss what our esteemed leader is about to reveal," said Madeleine.

"I assume by the smug look on your face that you have a revelation for us," Madeleine continued speaking to Tim.

"I have made a new friend called David Chan, not his real name of course. He is a Chinese spook and he had a little problem."

"The nature of this problem?" said Madeleine.

"He had had a bit of military hardware go missing but he doesn't know who took it or where it is."

"That's not our problem. Is it?" said Harriet.

"It sort of is," said Tim.

"What's missing," said Harriet.

"I'll come to that later."

"Building the dramatic tension?" said Madeleine.

Tim smiled. "So poor Mr Chan doesn't know who took it. Obviously it had to be someone high up in the military and part of or close to the pocket lining elite in power."

"Do we know who it is? Have I missed something?" said Madeleine.

"No we don't and you haven't. He had one lead a name, Somchai Onruang, who just shipped Jade to their unknown suspect."

"The same chap I linked via the money to the Dawar Corporation?" said Harriet.

"And the missing woman the police asked us if we could look into, Suzy Webb?" said Madeleine.

"The chap who was out in the cold, who came to me in Bangkok for shelter and who is now sadly deceased."

"Dead end then?" said Madeleine

"You are such a negative person," said Tim. "No, not at all a dead end in fact it is a new beginning. Mr Chan and I came to an arrangement. Would you like to hear it?"

"Stop pissing about," said Madeleine. Tim's original assessment that she was not in the best of humour was born out.

Tim ignored her. "I gave our friendly Chinese secret agent Ibrahim's details and told him all we found out about him, Somchai Onruang, Dawar and Mo the organiser of the terrorist plot here."

"You did what?"

"I let him know everything we held on these people at MI5."

"Are you supposed to do that? I mean it is sort of top secret and a bit treasonous helping a foreign power isn't it?" said Harriet.

"Well he did give me a really nice dinner at the Chinese Embassy in Bangkok."

"Of well that's alright then," said Madeleine.

"So the only question remains is why?" said Harriet. She knew from past experience that her boss had one of the sharpest and cunning minds of anyone she had ever met.

"The nice Chinese man has agreed to do all the work for us and work which we cannot undertake ourselves. It seems that they have a more laissez faire approach to human rights, than we do."

"Like imprisonment without trial and torture," said Harriet?

"Like we would never be a party to such thing, one word Guantanamo," retorted Madeleine.

"David Chan will contact Ibrahim Dawar in his own inimitable fashion and make detailed inquiries. He will share with us that which he discovers. I think Mr Chan will be extremely efficient in his endeavours and I anticipated that within twenty four hours we will know who and where our terrorist we called Mo is. I further anticipate that we will be able to tell the Police what happened to their ex-colleague Suzy Webb and the why. Hopefully the Chinese will get their weapon back and their thief and Jade smuggler."

"Well it sounds good to me," said Madeleine.

"There may be just one small problem," said Tim.

"What is that?"

"The missing Chinese weapon may be somewhere in the UK. If Mo or his merry band of Jihadis has it we could be facing a very nasty scenario."

"Right, what is the bit of missing military hardware?" said Madeleine.

Chapter 28

"But is it ready now?" Ibrahim was frantically speaking to Inglewood Aviation and one of the technicians. "Why has it taken so long?"

The exasperated voice came down the line. "First the electrics at the hanger could not have been re-wired since Noah set sail in the Ark. We have to have a reliable supply. Secondly to unpack and install with experienced personnel takes about eight hours with six men. There are two of us and thirdly the fucking instruction manuals are in Chinese. I speak English and Arabic. Is there anything about me that suggests to you that I might be Chinese?"

"Alright I get it," said Ibrahim.

"So let us know when and the target. We are ready."

Ibrahim put the phone down. He looked at the clock. Somewhere in England Mo would be entering a corner shop that allowed immigrants to the UK to make cheap international calls over the internet. to their country of origin to speak with their loved ones. The call would be only traceable back to the shop and by then Mo would be long gone.

He knew that Mo was likely to act rashly. The failure of the mass attack, the round up of the terror cells that he had spent so many years establishing and the seizure of the arsenal of weapons had been a big blow to him. He understood. They had sacrificed so much and tolled so hard to get it all together. They had been so close to unleashing the biggest terrorist attack in history on the UK only to be denied at the last.

He understood that it was only a matter of time before he, Mo and

Dawar would be linked. He had Somchai Onruang killed and that should buy some time. He knew they knew that the disappearance of Suzy Webb would eventually be traced back to Dawar. The smuggling of the Jade had his dealings with General Xi had been rash. He knew that. He also knew that the Chinese were not forgiving and he had trod on the toes of some of the most powerful oligarchs in that Country. It had been borne of desperation. Simply he had to go along with the Jade smuggling despite the probability that the Chinese, who held the monopoly on Jade from Burma, would find out as he had run out of money. As it turned out he got something better than money. He got the means to strike a real blow against the UK, an attack that would send shock waves around the World.

The clock ticked and the hands moved. The phone rang. He picked it up and put it to his ear. "Ibrahim," he said.

"I can wait no longer," Mo said. "The longer I wait the more I feel the noose tightening. I have waited far too long for revenge to let it slip from my grasp now."

"It is in place, please," he said. It was clear that Mo's mental state was far from rational. The stress, of all the years living in the shadows, avoiding detection by the British security services and recruiting all the members, for the cells up and down the Land, had taken its toll. It had been almost too much for him to bear when the weapons had been seized and his network destroyed.

"The British will be basking in their victory, patting themselves on the back for having taken down the biggest plot to date. While they are doing so, they will not expect what we have planned. We will catch them unprepared. We will hit them right at the centre. We will have our revenge," Ibrahim continued in the hope of calming him.

"I want to believe. I do. It has been so long coming. I pray each day to Allah for them. I pray for justice. I pray for them to be punished. I can pray no more I need to act."

"Wait it will come to pass. Believe me I have sacrificed everything to bring this about. It has sustained me all these years. We shall see justice."

"I know, I know but it has been so long. I fear I should forget."

"We will never forget. They will always be with us and in us. Now promise me you will wait? Now is not the time for rashness. You could destroy everything."

There was a long silence. "I have to go. I have been here on the phone too long already."

"Promise me"

"I promise," the phone line went dead.

Ibrahim replaced the receiver. He sat. There was no more to be done. He had to wait. He put he lights out as he left the Dawar building in Chiang Mai for the last time. He would disappear and return to Pakistan. He had passage booked.

He waked to the exit. The six men armed with machine pistols waited for him. He did not know how close the authorities were to him but he wanted to survive a little longer. He wanted to live long enough to read the headlines of the devastation in England. He wanted to relish the moment then he would be happy to die. They could do what they will then and only then.

He had bribed the Thai police to turn a blind eye. They were not the threat. He knew the British were sniffing at his heals. He feared that they would try and take him. That would now be very difficult. His escort were all ex military and fanatical in their beliefs. They would fight to the death.

Ibrahim has under estimated his foe. Tim Burr knew that he would never have official sanction to stage an operation on Thai soil. The authorities would never let UK Special Service kidnap and kill anyone however dangerous under their jurisdiction. There were many ways to skin a cat though. David Chan was the one Tim had chosen to skin his particular cat. That cat in the form of Ibrahim was leaving his headquarters at that exact moment.

The Chinese had none of the qualms of the British in violating Thai Sovereign territory. David knew that if he failed in finding the traitor who had imported the Jade and sold Chinese military hardware, he would find himself no longer in the land of the living. The Burmese military, which were in partnership with the Chinese oligarchs running Jade, had been instrumental in getting David's men into Thailand.

As Ibrahim and his bodyguard stepped from the building in the early hours they could not have imagined what awaited them. There was only the sound of what appeared to be loud coughing. The six men guarding Ibrahim fell dead as the David's snipers acquired their targets and fired.

At first Ibrahim was confused. He thought that his guard was performing some sort of tactical rehearsal. They just seemed to fall to the ground remaining motionless. Only slowly did it sink in that they were shot. They had all taken shots to the head killing them instantly. He stared into the darkness around him uncomprehending. The Chinese hit squad had no such problems seeing wearing night vision equipment.

David Chan stepped into the light. "Mr Dawar, it is nice to meet you. We are going to have a little chat, you and I. You are going to tell me everything. "

Ibrahim sought to run but as they the group of Chinese forces revealed themselves he knew that there was nowhere to run. "I will tell you nothing," he said.

"I understand you point of view but I think that at some stage you will change your mind. We find that a combination of drugs and torture usually persuades people to become extremely forthcoming in a very short time. We after all want very little from you, just a name. The name of the person you delivered the Jade to? Not so much to ask is it?"

Their conversation was cut short. The sound of helicopter rotor blades filled the darkness. They had flown across the border low circumnavigating Thailand's rudimentary defence systems. With the blessing of the Miramar military there was no hindrance to their passage.

Within moments the Chinese Special forces, the bodies of Ibrahim's bodyguards, David Chan and Ibrahim Dower were airborne. They would all vanish leaving no trace of what had occurred.

Chapter 29

Tim sat in Madeleine's office with Harriet. They waited eagerly for his reply.

"Stop building the tension," said Harriet. "What weapon have the Chinese lost track of?"

Tim smiled and said, "A drone."

"Why are you smiling? For fucks sake a drone. That is serious. Is it in the UK yet?" said Madeleine.

"I know it's serious and I have already alerted the air force and navy. Now we know the danger it is a significantly less of a threat. It has the full kit and caboodle, missiles, laser guidance and twenty four hour flying capability but we have a pretty good detection system for this type of threat."

"But it is still a significant threat."

"True but as they say forewarned is forearmed. We know what to expect so I am told there is a ninety five per cent probability it will be detected and destroyed within thirty minutes of launch."

"That still leaves five per cent of innocent people being killed on the streets," said Madeleine.

"It was one hundred per cent before I went to Bangkok and we knew nothing of the threat. Now the odds are stacked in our favour. Please do not forget the odds we are taking about are if it gets airborne. It won't get that far."

"Why is that?" said Harriet.

"The Chinese Government will do all they can to prevent it. Having one of their drones attack the UK is not on their 'to do' list. I feel my new found friend, Mr David Chan will pull out all the stops to stop it dead in its tracks," said Tim.

"So what do we do in the mean time?"

"You make your speech claiming credit for the taking down of Mo's multiple terrorist cells. Then you argue for more funding for the Departments vital roll in combating terrorism. In the meantime we trust to this Country's military to do their job and take out the drone if they get it up and flying," said Tim.

*****

David Chan was becoming impatient. The sound of screaming was making him uncomfortable. Fundamentally he was a soldier not a torturer. He knew that it was vital that they broke Ibrahim quickly. The loss of profit to the Chinese elite that controlled the Jade trade was now secondary to locating the missing drone.

The large sweaty faced Captain entered his office. He looked tired from his efforts. "Well," asked David?

"He is fanatical. He would rather die that cooperate."

"Why are you here then? I need answers and I need them fast."

"I have established with the polygraph that in all likelihood he does not know the current location of the drone. It is somewhere in the UK but he isn't lying when he says he doesn't know its exact whereabouts. I believe him. He funded the operation but deliberately kept himself out of the detail guarding against the situation he is now in."

"Okay so we need to know who he smuggled the Jade for. We need that name. He is the key. He traded the drone for the Jade. He has to know where it was delivered."

"You will have the name in the hour, trust me. I am just taking a break while the drugs kick in. He is not a young man. We do not want to kill him that would serve no purpose."

The Captain lit a cigarette and pored himself a cup of tea. He checked his watch several times before eventually rising, left the room and returned to his task of torturing Ibrahim. "No rest for the wicked, hey?" he said as he departed.

David sat tense as the screaming began again. It was a sound he hoped never to hear again. He had seen the equipment that was now being used on the unfortunate. Some were crude items, pliers and an even a cheese grater others were sophisticated, a high voltage generator with a probe attached for the anus and penis for example. There was also an array of medical equipment and drugs.

Finally the screaming stopped. The silence was more intimidating than Ibrahim's pain. The door opened. The Captain entered, stripped to the waste. His body was bathed in sweat. "I have never come across some one so determined. He was filled with hate and insane with the lust for revenge."

"Was" said David picking up on the Captain's use of the past tense?

"He has passed..."

"He's dead. Did you get the name?"

"Please I am a professional. He would not be dead if we did not have what we wanted."

******

The Casino in the Venetian Hotel in Macao was packed. Time stood still inside its palatial confines. There were no clocks and the passing of day and night, were ignored. It was fantasy Venice complete with

Canals and gondoliers, churches and palaces replanted in the East. For the gamblers it was a self contained World dedicated to gambling.

The high rollers were treated like royalty, complimentary drinks, food, accommodation and any type of sexual activity that meet their desires were all served around the clock. It was a casino with a hotel. It was a money extraction machine, which keep giving as long as the client kept losing.

General Xi was a high roller. He had a Vietnamese passport and spoke only French the language he had studied at University in Beijing before joining the army. His father had been part of the ruling military elite and party member until a change in the Countries leadership had swept him away. But things change and another change saw the family back in favour and Xi took his rightful place in the army. He did not forget however. He had no loyalty to the Chinese Communist Party.

He had made himself useful, rose through the ranks and found his niche bringing in Jade from Burma for the ruling oligarchs. He only received a pittance for his pains compared to his billionaire masters. He wanted more.

Then it had all come together for him, the stock pile of jade held by the Burmese rebels, the fanatic Ibrahim and the deal to steal the drone. He was the right person in the right place. It was a once in a life time opportunity. He had grasped it with both hands. He had paid a fraction of the Jades real value to the rebels. Ibrahim cost him nothing just the stroke of a pen and a Chinese drone disappeared. Xi was now a billionaire and Ibrahim had his weapon of mass destruction in England.

Xi was feeling on top of the world as he made his way to the lift. Even his losses at the tables had not affected his mood. Two hundred thousand dollars was chicken fed to him now and there were compensations. One was the beautiful blond with a perfect body who he had met earlier. He had given her the key to his suite and she was waiting for him. Unlucky at the tables but lucky in love, he thought as he rode the elevator,

He opened the door to the room. It was dark inside. As he reached for the light switch he expected to see the naked woman waiting in his bed. He saw nothing as David Chan's team seized him and injected the sedative.

Chapter 30

The knocking on the door at Inglewood Aviation refused to go away. "You will have to answer it," said the first technician.

"If we wait they will surely get fed up and go away," came the reply.

They could hear voices outside the hanger, then banging on the hanger door. "That does not sound like someone about to go away. Does it? See what they want."

Reluctantly he made his way back into the office. They were both tired assembling the Chinese drone and calibrating everything had been harder than expected. They were both experienced operators but the Chinese version of its US counterpart, whilst similar had a few significant differences. They had encountered a major glitch in connecting to a satellite essential for communication, control and guidance. Eventually they had overcome the problem but not without a great deal of work and frustration. They were ready but tired hungry and wanted something to eat.

They were waiting on the green light and target from Ibrahim. No such green light was ever to be forthcoming. Ibrahim was already dead at the hands of his Chinese interrogators.

He walked to the door and unlocked it. Two agitated men were outlined against the grey blue sky as he pulled the door open. They seemed annoyed and immediately spoke. "This is no way to treat customers," one began.

"We are closed for refurbishment," said the technician.

"What? Look we booked this months ago with Red Voucher.com.

Here is the conformation from Inglewood."

He thrust a piece of paper into the technician's hand. He read. It was clearly what the man had said it was two prepaid trips in the vintage Tiger Moth, today and at Inglewood.

"Look we are not operating at the moment. You will have to re-book."

"That is not good enough. We have travelled up from London especially. It is my friend's birthday."

"There is nothing I can do." He tried to close the door.

The second man stepped forward and pushed past him into the office. Things were rapidly escalating with the disgruntled customers. He needed to do something to get rid of them before matters deteriorated.

"Perhaps a refund?" he said.

"And two complementary flights for our wasted journey?"

"Of course, now if you give me you account details I will arrange a transfer. It will take a few days."

"Do it now," the second customer now made his way into the office and closed the door behind him.

"I can't do it now I need the cahier to put through the..."

The sentence was never completed. The first irate customer had positioned himself directly behind the technician. He withdrew the specialist commando knife from its sheaf, which he worse below his left armpit, concealed beneath his jacket. It was razor Sharpe with a fine point and a serrated edge. It could stab easily penetrating through bone or cut smoothly through flesh. The man, he had been talking to watched dispassionately as his colleague drew the knife across his throat. He had grasped the hair on his head, pulling it back to expose the neck. The movement was swift and well rehearsed the cut quick and fatal, the blade so sharp that the head was almost severed from the body.

The first assassin stepped forward and caught the body as his associated released the hair to prevent the head coming away in his hand. He had no time to register what was happening to him. There was only the sound of a deep sigh, and a gurgle. He drowned in his own blood as he was gently lowered to the ground.

"Have you got rid of them?" came a voice from the hanger.

The two men did not respond. They located the staircase that led to the ground floor and the connecting door to the hanger. The moved without making a sound. Slowly but sure-footedly they descended to the source of the voice.

There was a small entrance from the toilet and kitchen area on the ground floor that joined to the adjacent hanger. The first man looked into the hanger. His view was obscured by the two vintage planes, a Piper and the Tiger Moth. To the front of the hanger, to his left was a more modern two seater Piper Airplane used for training.

Both men moved into the hanger proper and remained hidden behind the Tiger Moth. They were trying to determine how many personnel were in the hanger.

"Can you hear me?" The same voice called out.

They were satisfied that there was only one terrorist remaining. The used hand signals to organise their attack. One went to the rear and the other moved to block the man's escape through the hanger doors. Neither made a sound as they stalked their pray.

The first stepped into view. Now he was satisfied that all was to plan. There between him and the Jihadi, ready to fly was the missing drone. He had been unable to see it earlier. His view obscured by the two vintage plans.

The man became aware of his presence, despite the stealth of his movements. "You colleague said we could have a look at the Tiger

Moth." It was nonsense but it caused the terrorist to stop for an instant, while he processed the statement before turning to reach for the Uzi machine pistol that was on the bench beside him.

The assassins could have shot him but they wanted silence to prevail for as long as possible so they would be distant, before someone came to investigate the sound of gunshots.

The hesitation was just enough to allow the second man to step forward and use his knife. He thrust the blade in at the base of the spine and severed the spinal column paralyzing him form the waist down. As he collapsed, his head was pulled back and his jugular vein cut. He convulsed and died.

The two men made a sweep of the hanger. Satisfied that there were no other occupants, they made their way back up the stairs to the office and the first corpse. They picked the body up and took it back down into the hanger laying it alongside the other deceased.

"What's that smell?"

They had both become aware of the sickly, pungent aroma that was present in the hanger. They were battle hardened enough to recognise it, human decomposition.

"It's here." They had located the murdered body of the previous owner of the flying school, Gerald Inglewood. His body had been pushed into a large packing box that was beginning to leek the bodily fluids into a small pool around it. They terrorists considered that they would be long gone and clear before the police located the hanger and the source of the drone strike. There was no need to incur the risk of disposing of his body and possible detection whilst doing so.

The two assassins pulled the box across they hanger floor and placed it next to the two other bodies. One waited while the other went back up through the office and out to the car in which they had arrived. He was aware of the CCTV cameras on the adjacent industrial and warehousing complex and so as on arrival he avoided his face being captured.

He returned to the hanger with the explosives. They worked efficiently, practiced as a team to rig the hanger. It took less than five minutes and they were driving away. The car they were in was registered to a fake address and owner. The car they pulled up alongside parked off road on a quiet wooded area was also untraceable.

The waited until the first car was fully ablaze destroying any forensic evidence that would link them to its capture on CCTV before they drove off.

Clear of the burning car the passenger pulled his cell phone from his pocket and dialled. A phone rang once in the hanger and triggered the bomb. The blast was huge and could be heard for over three miles around, in the quiet Sussex countryside. Hanger planes drone and bodies were destroyed beyond recognition. Only a crater remained. No one was injured avoiding any unwelcome complications.

David Chan received a phone call as they made their way to Heathrow and the plane to Beijing.

Chapter 31

"Welcome back to England Phillip," said Tim.

"It was a surprise and a promotion, thank you," said Phillip Hetherington. They were sitting in the lobby of the Monmouth Hotel, a short walk from Cambridge Circus and venue of the ever running musical, Les Miserables.

"Well," said Tim. "I am not feeling one hundred percent yet and not fully back at work. I need someone to do the odd bit of running about for me. You seem to have proved yourself in that area when I was in Thailand."

"Well thank you anyway. I was happy in Bangkok but it did not hold out much in terms of career opportunities. That's for sure. At least here I can prove my worth."

"Okay just don't get too enthusiastic. If I hear the phrase, "I am passionate about," marketing, flower selling or dog shit, I shall lose the will to live," said Tim.

Phillip Laughed. "I'll tone it down. I promise."

"Good, remember this is not an episode of the Apprentice and I am not Donald Trump. Just do as required, no initiative required at this stage. In this job lack of initiative can equal longevity. Now let me be clear. You have undergone field training and unlike me you actually know one end of a gun from the other?"

"I was in the army first. I went to Sand Hurst and passed out before someone suggested a career change." Sand Hurst was the Army Officer training college.

"Someone in MI5?"

"MI6 actually but I got sidetrack and ended up in MI5,"

"Happens to the best of us," Tim laughed as recalled how he had ended up as Director General. "Any way I am officially off on sick leave and as you know Madeleine Wilson is acting head at the moment."

"So I am official but not officially working at MI5?" Phillip looked puzzled.

"You are helping me. I have booked you a room here. You will find your paperwork, your gun and ammunition in it."

"Will I need it?" Phillip looked concerned.

"I am not sure. I think I have managed to put together most of the pieces from my visit in Bangkok but there is something missing. I fear that the missing piece may well turn out to be the most difficult to remove from the board, using a chess analogy. "

"I don't understand?"

"The common element that remains constant is a terrorist we have named Mo. He seems to have beavered away under the radar for years. We were tracking a terrorist cell in Luton when he first turned up. He led us to other cells around the Country. He was then linked to the financing via our friends at Dawar in Thailand. He then turns up when we raid a lockup, where a load of arms are being stored. He escapes by detonating a bomb and shoots his way clear."

"And he is still out there somewhere. Do you know who he is?"

"Not one hundred per cent, Harriet Shaw is doing a bit of digging for me. She is trying to put together some family trees of Pakistani immigrants to the UK. It is difficult but she has people working on it over there as well. In the mean time and If I am right he is on a mission to get revenge and has a specific target. I just don't have all the pieces yet, as I said before."

"What have the Chinese to do with all this? When you went missing in Thailand you told me you had dinner with them."

"That was a money raising exercise by Dawar. They organised a bit of Jade smuggling to fund the terrorists here in the UK. A Chinese General got fed up of doing all the work for the elite oligarchs enriching themselves, while he got scrapes. He decided to go into business himself. He did a deal with Dawar, whereby they got a bucket load of Jade worth millions from Burmese rebels and smuggled it to China for him."

"That chap that got murdered in Bangkok, how did he fit in?"

"Somchai Onruang, he was the link between Dawar and the Jade smuggling General. The Dawar Corporation, or Ibrahim to be more precise, had him removed from the board in an attempt to cover up the link," said Tim.

"So what, the only piece left in play is this terrorist Mo?"

"I hope so. Well apart from the fact the Chinese told me, that one of their drones has gone missing. "

"Drone as in military type drone, as in laser targeting, missile firing, big explosion, building reduced to smithereens, carnage type drone?" said Phillip.

"Yes that would be it, one of those. I am pretty sure it was flown, as airfreight to England. "

"Where is it?"

"Well I am hoping that the Chinese have sorted it out for me. There was a report of massive explosion at a Sussex based private flying school on the news. I have a meeting arranged with the Chinese later. Again I am hoping that will clarify matters somewhat."

Tim's phone rang. "Harriet, what have you found out?" There was a brief pause as Tim listened. "I thought there would be a connection. Well done, just keep it to yourself for the present."

Phillip looked at Tim. "Well," he said?

"I think I know who Mo is but I don't know where. We will have his passport in a few hours and then his photograph will be circulated Nationwide. Hopefully he will be picked up on CCTV somewhere and facial recognition software will do its job."

"Do we know his target?"

"I haven't quite worked that bit out yet," said Tim.

"So what shall I be doing?"

"You will be tracking down our recalcitrant terrorist. If I am right he will pop up sooner rather than later with the intention of killing somebody. It is his last chance to cause a bit of misery. He is on his own now as far as we know. The terror cells have been taken down. The imported arms have been seized. His source of finance has been cut off and hopefully the Chinese have recovered or destroyed their errant drone."

"What all on my own?"

"You are being a bit silly now," said Tim.

"Sorry," Phillip looked a little abashed.

"You will focus on the information from GCHQ. They will track all electronic communication from him. I am hoping that after my meeting with the Chinese will have a phone, an email address, a server or some identifier that GCHQ can put an alert on. MI5, the police and the Police Counter Terrorism units nationwide will be watching CCTV and number plates for him. Sooner or later he will come up. You will be there where and whenever he pops his head up."

Chapter 32

Madeleine Wilson was showing signs of panic at Thames House. Her aids and secretaries were rushing about in all directions. A note had arrived from the Home Secretary. The Home Secretary was the new Home Secretary and had been in the job less than twelve hours. The previous Home Sectary who had been in the job less than a month had followed her predecessor by resigning over the Prime Minister's plans to extract the UK from the European Union, known as Brexit.

In attempt to sell her so called Brexit Agreement with the EU to the Country and her fellow Members of Parliament, who would eventually vote on it, the PM was on a charm offensive. One of the perceived strengths of the latest plan was the continued security cooperation between the member States of the European Union. MI5 credit taking speech for its success against the terrorist cells and arms seizures was to be reworked into a eulogy praising the role of the UK's counterparts in the EU and emphasising how these close links would be continued under the PM's Brexit agreement with the EU.

MI5, in form of Madeleine, was to be wheeled out to stress the continued importance of EU cooperation in safeguarding the safety of the UK. Sadly the speech Madeleine had intended to make had nothing on the particular subject that the new Home Secretary found so compelling.

"Give me the latest draft," said Madeleine. She read. "No we have to mention the Germans some where in it and their importance."

She handed the speech back for more drafting. She looked at her watch. Time was running out. She had to appear on the steps of the Mansion House with the PM in under two hours. The Mansion House was the official residence of the Lord Mayor of London. The Lord Mayor was not to be confused with the elected Mayor of London. The former was an unpaid position dating back hundreds of years and represented the interests of the businesses that thrived in the square mile known as the City.

The new Mayor held office for a period of twelve months. The Lord Mayor's Parade, a pageant of pomp and circumstance had taken place earlier that day. The City were in the main behind the Prime Ministers Plan for leaving the EU as it meant almost no change to the existing trade arrangements with the rest of the Countries in the European Union. No change and business as usual was fine for business.

The new Lord Mayor, a leading financier and a staunch opponent of leaving the European Economic Union had taken the unusual step of sharing the limelight of his appointment celebrations by tagging on a quasi promotional event on the steps of the Mansion House backing the PM. Madeleine along with other prominent figures were being rolled out to extol the virtues of the Agreement reached with the EU for the UK's exit.

"You know this is a security nightmare," said Harriet.

"Yes I do. The police personal protection, us, Counter Terror and MI6 are falling over one another. What can we do? It is so last minute there is no time to coordinate."

"The area will be packed with tourists and bystanders who came out to watch the Lords Mayor's Parade. The head of security really wants to sit down with you and review the arrangements. He is not a very happy person. He says that it is a real mess."

"Tell him sorry. I haven't the time. Tell him to do his best," said Madeleine as she was handed what seemed like the thousandth re-draft of her speech." She began to read.

"Right," said Harriet. "I'll do my best."

"Nice to see you again," said David Chan.

"Nice not to be abducted," said Tim. He had arrived at the Chinese Embassy in Portland Place under his own steam on this occasion.

"Can I get you some refreshment?"

"I think time is not with us. Can we get down to business?

"Of course, you will be glad that we have been as good as our word In Bangkok," said David.

"I am glad to hear it."

"We picked up Ibrahim as you advised. He was a bit reluctant to talk but he did eventually. You were right. He and Dawar were funding the plots in the UK. As you know he led us to our Jade smuggling and drone stealing General. He gave us the location of the drone here in the UK. The threat to your Country has now been removed."

"The explosion at the airfield?" said Tim.

"No more drone and no more terrorists that is apart from one."

"I think we know his identity but not his location," said Tim.

"We may be able to help with the latter," said David. He handed a mobile phone to Tim. "Ibrahim's phone, he still had it on him when he became our guest."

"Thank you, we will get straight on it." Tim rose to leave and extended his hand.

"I have one more gift for you. We were very thorough in our search of Ibrahim and also his office and residence. We found this." He gave Tim the memory stick.

"What is it?"

"It contains some video footage. It appears to have been shot on an early camera phone. It is about ten years old. You should watch it."

****

Mo sat watching the television as the Lord Mayor's Parade started out. He was worried. No contact from Dawar had increased his anxiety levels. The last communication he had with Ibrahim had reassured him that the drone was soon to be ready for action. He was expecting to be contacted by the drone pilots. Nothing from them either. He had no way of knowing that Ibrahim and been captured by the Chinese, tortured and was now dead. He had no way of knowing that Ibrahim had given up General xi. Who was, also tortured and killed. He had no way of knowing that general Xi had given up the location of the drone, the two pilots and that they had been murdered and the drone blown to pieces by Chinese Intelligence. What he was beginning to know was that he was on his own, the last man standing.

The drone had been his and Ibrahim's ultimate revenge. It would have flown to the Capital and wrecked death and destruction on a scale not seen since World War II and the bombing of London by the Luft Waffe. It was to target MI5 HQ, MI6 and the Police Counter Intelligence and its final strike would have been ten Downing Street, the Prime Ministers Residence.

He had to know. He dialled Ibrahim's cell. The norm had been to both use single use unregistered cell phones and destroy them after they had spoken. This made it almost impossible to track the users. The new number would be tweeted on a series of accounts that could be viewed with out signing up to the app. New phones and new numbers each call was almost impossible to trace.

Now desperate, with no new tweets left Mo with no means of communicating. He had to know what was happening. He knew it was a small risk but even so he hesitated. He had remained off the radar for nearly ten years. He realised he had run out of options.

He took his mobile and dialled. It connected to the last phone number he had for Ibrahim. It went to voice mail. Ibrahim had probably disposed of it. Mo had no other way to make contact. He left a voice mail.

Phillip Hetherington's cell phone rang. It was GCHQ.

Chapter 33

The Prime Minister was due to arrive. She was to be accompanied by the latest Foreign Secretary. The Mansion House steps were a mass of jostling journalists fighting to get their stills and videos clips. There were two groups of protestors marching, one from the east and the other from the west. The remainers were descending on the City from the east and the leavers from European Union from the opposite direction. The Metropolitan Police and the City Police were working together to avoid a head on clash.

The agreement to exit the European Union would have to be put before Parliament soon. The general feeling among MPs was that it was a bad deal. Neither the pro leave nor the pro remain members liked it. The Prime Minister was in a last ditch stand to garner support for the exit deal, which she had negotiated with the European Union.

Her appearance at the Lord Mayor's Parade was one of many personal appearances, along with countless television and radio interviews that had been crammed in to promote the deal. It was a difficult time for the security services with feelings running high and so many events stretching their resources.

The UK population could not carry guns unlike their cousins across the pond in the US. Whilst not facing the same level of risk of motiveless mass shootings the UK was still vulnerable to terrorist attack and individuals using vehicles or knives as weapons. Imported guns were in the main being using by criminals in the drug trade with no specific political agenda.

The difficulty of obtaining guns by the British public meant that the focus of the security forces attention was on the latest preferred method used by extremists to kill, that of high jacking a truck and driving it into crowds of innocent people. Only weeks before a four by four had been driven into the pedestrians on Westminster Bridge killing many before being crashed into the barriers at the Houses of Parliament. The driver had leapt from the vehicle and stabbed an unarmed policeman before the armed response unit had shot and killed him.

The City of London had what was described as a ring of steel around it. It was recognised that the centre of the Country's banking and financial services sector was a serious target for terrorists. The ring of steel had been put in place during the Irish Troubles. It was literally what its name suggested. The roads in and out had barriers of reinforced steel buffers erected across them. Traffic was forced to stop and vehicles could be searched. In addition CCTV monitored the movements of every vehicle that entered the cordon. ANPR technology tracked every vehicle's registration and immediately flagged to the Police any car, truck or taxi that was unregistered or had been flagged for previous suspicious activity.

Madeleine and Harriet arrived. MI5 were doing their part in the surveillance stakes. Agents were in the crowds of protestors, some under cover some had just joined the crowds for the day's marches. It was arguable that the groups of protestors would have been considerably smaller without the number of Intelligence personal from all the various Agencies swelling their ranks.

"This is madness," said Madeleine as they exited the car. "Look at it families and spectators for the Lord Mayor's Parade, tourists and protesters drawn by the PM's appearance."

"Don't forget the Jihadi still on the loose. We can't rule that out either as a threat."

"Here comes the PM's advanced personal protection unit. A police van pulled up and more police joined the conflagration.

"She must be on her way. You had better get yourself up on the steps. Have you got your speech?" said Harriet.

"I am not happy about this. I don't think it is MI5's job to support a particular politician or political party."

"No its not and you aren't. Our job is to keep the Country safe, a no deal Brexit would mean a chaotic uncertain situation between us and our European partner agencies. You can argue quite legitimately for the need for seamless cooperation between us and Europe's secret services. That is not politically partisan," said Harriet.

"I know but it doesn't sit well and all of this feels a bit like a circus." She said as she made her way up the steps to join the throng waiting for the Prime Minister's arrival.

Mo had joined the mass of protestors and tourists entering the City. He had been concerned that the rifle would be a magnet for security and surveillance. He had just made a placard, wrapped the gun in paper and used the gun as the handle. The placard read 'Security first stay in the EU'. The gun looked liked a cleverly fashioned handle to the banner in the shape of a rifle.

He knew it was madness but no one noticed him among the thousands of marchers. Many had banners far more elaborate. A group of Scottish fishermen, who were leavers, had a giant cod as a protest against their fishing grounds being accessed by foreign fishing fleets. Giant walking strawberries were representing fruit growers that wanted to remain and have access to cheap EU labour to pick their crops. As Madeleine had rightly observed it was a circus.

It was chaotic and Mo could not believe that the police had established two cordoned off areas in front of that Mansion House, one for pro and one for anti Brexit protestors. The British right to peaceful protest and assembly was working to his full advantage. He had been positioned with a perfect view, where in a few moments the Prime Minister would be on public display. He would only have to step from the crowd and fire his automatic assault riffle. He would die of course but so would his target. Mo did not want to live. He had only continued living in anticipation of this moment. He stood in the crowd with his riffle banner waving and waited for his chance. He moved steadily to the front and edged nearer to the steps of the Mansion House. He broke the wrapping around the trigger of the gun. He would just lower it and point. It did not matter that taped to the end was a cardboard placard. It would, in now way prevent the rifle from spraying death. This close aiming was not an issue. He would point and fire. As long as his target was killed a few more deaths were of no consequence.

Phillip Hetherington knew that his terrorist was among the crowd somewhere. His phone put him in the area. Tim had been right. He had directed him to focus on Mo and let the rest of the Service concentrate on protection. He was here to hunt and they were here to defend.

The facial recognition software was trolling through images for the crowd and the protestors. It had a lot to process. Finally the words arrived in Phillip's ear piece. "He is in the protestors in front of the Mansion House Steps."

He had been stood in front of the Royal Exchange opposite the Bank of England. He ran towards the corralled protestors. Logic dictated that his target would be to the front affording him the best chance of killing the Prime Minister. Phillip began to desperately push his way through to the front. Mo was stood at the back and Phillip passed within feet of him.

The Prime Minister's cavalcade arrived. Her close protection unit appeared from all directions and her personal bodyguard remained glued to her side. They all knew that Brexit was dividing the Nation and in that atmosphere extremists saw opportunity. Phillip turned his back and faced the crowd. He frantically scanned the crowd for his target.

With flashing lights from the photographers and a barrage of cameras and lights before her the Prime Minister began to speak. The speech was targeted as much at her own Members of Parliament that she feared would rebel against her in the House of Commons, as it was addressed to the Nation. Her message was any deal with the European Union was better than leaving with a no deal. It was not scanning well with either the leavers or the remainers.

She had her list of speakers paraded each in turn stressing the need for continued cooperation with the EU. Eventually Madeleine Wilson acting Deputy General of MI5 was called on to make her contribution. Phillip watched the crowd but could not spot his suspect.

The speaking came to an end and after a well set piece plea by the PM for the Country to unite behind her negotiated exit agreement. She started to descend the steps to the waiting car. This would bring her as close to the mob as she had been so far. Philip felt the tension rise. It was now or never for Mo to act.

Nothing, no movement no attack, the PM got in the Ministerial Car and drove off accompanied by the Police cavalcade. Phillip relaxed. Madeleine and Harriet stood at the top of the steps. "Nothing," said Madeleine.

"I don't understand. Tim is rarely wrong. He always is one step ahead."

As if on cue, Harriet's phone rang. "It's Tim," said Harriet.

She struggled to hear him above the still chanting protestors. "The target .."

She moved her position, "say again."

"The target is not the PM..."

Mo stepped forward and began firing. Bullets ricocheted off the pillars of the Mansion House portico. He sprayed the group that remained.

The security personnel had relaxed after the Prime Minister's departure, seeing the threat as passed. Their attention diverted they were slow to react. Mo had been able to move easily to the fore as the crowd begin to leave after the Prime Minister, the focus of the anger had departed. He had knelt pointed his placard disguised gun and pulled the trigger.

Philip was still on alert. He saw the threat and pulled his gun. He fired once. He did not miss. He stood to the left of Mo and the bullet entered his temple killing him instantly. He approached the body and despite the accuracy of the shot, he held his gun on the body and kicked it, checking for signs of life.

"Tim," Phillip said into the small microphone on his lapel. "He's dead. It's over."

Chapter 34

Tim sat watching the live television coverage from the steps of the Mansion House, in the City of London. The reporters were held well back from the actual scene of the shootings but in the background as they did their pieces to camera, could be seen the array of ambulances and police cars attending. Sirens could be heard as ambulance after ambulance rushed the injured to hospital.

On what was to have been a declaration of success in the breaking up of a terror network by the Intelligence Community, was now an exposure of the vulnerability of the Nation's defences to such acts.

The attack was being widely reported as an attempted assassination of the Prime Minister. The fact that it had failed to kill her was being touted as some sort of success. The Government spin doctors were already at work putting a positive narrative on the events.

Tim felt sickened by the media manipulation unfolding. The remain in the European Union lobby, was claiming how much worse it could have been without EU cooperation. The leavers were shouting that tighter immigration would stop terrorist being in the Country in the first place. The Police responsible for the PM's personal protection were claiming a success. Leading Muslim clerics were busy distancing themselves from the killings as not being representative of the Community as a whole. ISIS, the fundamentalist Islamic group was busy claiming responsibility.

Tim knew that all of the above were untrue. He replayed the footage found on Ibrahim memory stick. He was saddened by what he saw. A decision that was made many years earlier had resulted in such a cost. The reports of the deaths and those critically injured kept being revised but only in an upward direction. The assault riffle used by Mo had been fully automatic and the extended magazine had been fully fired into the crowd congregated on the steps. Six were reported dead so far and the injured could number further eight to twelve. More would die from their wounds.

As Tim sat numbed by the scenes unfolding on the TV and the intelligence reports being fed to his computer screen, the door opened. Madeleine was clearly in a state of shock. She made no comment that Tim has resumed his Chair, as Director General. He looked at her as she sat trembling on the leather sofa by the coffee table.

He stood up from behind the desk, crossed the room and sat beside her. "You still don't know what this is about, do you?"

She looked at him confused. She had expected a sympathetic shoulder. What she got was a very unsympathetic Tim. "I don't understand..." she began to speak.

"Let me help you. Let's go back to two thousand and five, thirteen years ago. You were forty one years of age and you were seconded to the Police training college in Hendon."

2005

It was a bright August morning as Madeleine Wilson breathed a sigh of relief and pulled into the car park at Hendon. The traffic had been worse than usual on the North Circular, the inner ring round around London. She had thought that she had allowed plenty of time but now had to gather he notes and rush to the lecture room.

The class were already seated as she entered. They rose as she came into the room. She gestured for them to resume their seats. Apologizing for being late she loaded her slides into the overhead projector. The assembled were not new recruits. They were experienced serving officers

Madeleine was making her career in the Specialist Operations directorate, a unit of the Metropolitan Police Service. Her job at Hendon was part education and part recruitment. More armed and trained officers were needed on the Street of the Capital and across the Country as a whole. In addition more focused training was needed in detecting and dealing with the rising terror threats in the UK and across the World. The course was two weeks in length and run every three months. The duties of running it were spread around the serving officers in the SO unit. It was Madeleine's turn to run the course.

Madeleine enjoyed the break and put her efforts fully into engaging with the other officers on the course. She was, if the truth be told lonely. After her partner had left her for another woman the previous year she had given up on finding the 'right one' and become career focused.

She and Anne had been together over eleven years. Madeleine had not seen it coming. They had even discussed having a baby. With hindsight, she realised that she had put too much pressure on the relationship. She had assumed that Anne would be happy to be pregnant and give up her work as a telesales operator, while Madeleine continued in her job with the Police.

She had been selfish, taking Anne for granted. She had undervalued her partner's contribution to the relationship. Now she understood but at the time she had been absorbed in her view of life. She would focus on her ambition to rise in the ranks while Anne would provide the home and family.

"Hi," the young woman" had said approaching Madeleine in the car park. "Are you stuck?"

"It won't start. I am waiting for the AA to send some one." Madeleine had replied.

The conversation developed. It had plenty of time to develop. The repair truck took an hour and a half to turn up. Finally Madeleine's car was up and running.

"Can I give you a lift?"

They had gone for a meal before she drove her home. Madeleine could tell she was about ten years younger than her but she felt a real connection with her. She was happy when they shared a kiss. It was a gentle kiss that spread warmth as well as desire. There was something special between them.

Life changed over the next two years. Madeleine found love again. They moved into together and Madeleine's promotions came thick and fast. Her partner joined the Counter Terror Armed Response unit at her urging.

2007

"Big day, first out in your new role," said Madeleine.

Suzy hugged her. "I must admit I am nervous."

"Just remember your training and follow procedure. You will be fine. Don't forget I am at the other end of the radio link heading up Command and Control. Trust me you will be brilliant." Madeleine gave her a big kiss and hug.

The raid on the Mosque in London's East End did not go well from the beginning. The building plans were out of date. The Police officers were becoming disorientated in the building and lacked coordination. In Command and Control the picture relayed back was becoming more and more confused. Uncertainty and lack of clarity on the ground was causing a breakdown of communication and fragmentation.

"There's been a shot fired." Madeleine heard the Officer shout. She left her position and checked the situation. She realised that the officer responsible was her lover. She took change of her feed.

"Talk to me," she said calmingly, realising that Suzy was panicking. She told her to switch channels taking their conversation private.

"I think I killed someone." the trembling voice into Madeleine's earpiece responded.

Madeleine felt her stomach knot. She reacted instinctively as a lover not as a Policeman. "Seal the scene. Keep everyone out. I'll be there and take control."

She made one excursion for leaving. In her office there was evidence that had not yet been logged or put in storage. Part of the evidence was the gun. She pulled the thick plastic bag open and took it out. She would later ensure that the whole file and allied exhibits became lost. It was to be some lucky criminal's day when later the police could not produce the evidence against him in Court.

"Charles, have you kept the scene sealed?" she said to Suzy's partner as she entered the room above the Mosque where Javeria Kathia lay dead at Suzy's hand.

"No one has been in," he affirmed.

Madeleine quickly took in her surroundings. Javeria lay dead in a pool of blood and Suzy seemed welded to the spot, in a state of shock. "Go and take Charles with you. Tell him to get Scene of Crime here."

Suzy hesitated.

"Go now," she said.

Alone Madeleine placed the gun in Javeria's hand, looked around then left the room and waited outside for forensics to arrive.

Chapter 35

Life in Pakistan was never easy. There were two very unremarkable sisters Mina and Sami Dawar. They were part of a hardworking and religious family. Their parents found them good husbands from their own caste. Sami married her husband, Mehmet Bukhari and moved to England. Mina married Ibrahim Kathia and remained in Pakistan, where he had a small quarry mining for nephrite jade.

They were happy and they had children. Sami's son was Reza and Mina had a daughter Javeria. There was a long tradition among Pakistanis to marry their first cousins. In England as high as fifty percent did so. Part tradition and part pragmatism ensued that the practice continues. The caste system is far more entrenched in Pakistan than in neighbouring India. Marrying outside you caste can lead to becoming ostracized by the community and shame. The other driver for marrying a first cousin is that wealth is kept in the family

In two thousand and seven Ibrahim Kathia put his wife Mina, his daughter, Javeria and his sister in law, Sami on a plane to England. He would never see his wife and daughter again.

He believed in British justice and knew that there was no way that Javeria was a terrorist. Of course neither he nor his wife, her sister or her intended husband Reza Bukhari could have know that the Police Officer in Charge would fake the evidence to protect her lover, Suzy Webb.

When Mina's mother killed herself Ibrahim was left with nothing but hate and a small box of Mina's meagre possession, including her cell phone. Reza was left with nothing but the loss of the woman he loved and the stigma her being labelled of terrorist. Neither had any form of justice from the British. The daughter and lover had been murdered and they were left with lies.

Reza and Ibrahim found solace in their mutual hatred. The hatred over the years turned to extremism and fundamentalism fuelled by the West's persecution of their Muslim brothers around the World. Revenge became their obsession and their driving force.

Ibrahim adopted his wife's maiden name, Dawar for himself and his business and so obscured the obvious link to his dead daughter. He worked hard, grew his business and channelled the money to fund terrorism in the UK. Reza, known to MI5 as Mo built his contacts and built up his network of terrorist cells. They had no specific target. They just planned to attack the police and the Counter Terror unit specifically, which had been the actual murderers of Javeria.

Ibrahim then made his contact with General Xi and his business jumped a league and he expanded into Thailand. The time was nearly upon him and Reza, time for revenge.

Then it all had come tumbling down. One mistake and Mo, Reza had been unearthed by a Mi5 surveillance team in Luton by visiting a group on the Watch List. The terrorist cells that had taken Reza years to build were taken down. The weapons intended to be used were then seized and Reza just managed to escape the raid on the lockup.

It looked like all the planning and years of work had been wasted. Then General Xi had offered the drone for the Jade if Ibrahim could get it out of Burma and into Hong Kong. They could still get their revenge. They would launch the drone and target the Police, MI5 and cause as many deaths and as much destruction as they could before it would eventually be taken out by the British Air force.

In all those years Ibrahim had not been able to bring himself to open his wife's meagre belongings, which her sister had returned to him after she committed suicide. It was now time with his and Reza's revenge at hand to do so. It was sad. He cried as he picked over the contents of the cardboard box, a few photos, some invitations for his daughter's wedding, clothes and an old Nokia camera phone.

He found the charger in the box and turned the phone on hoping to see some photos of his wife and daughter in England. He did but he also found the video clip of the firearms officer that had murdered his daughter and got away with it. The clip Mina had taken from the toilet window at the Coroner's inquest, when Suzy had given her evidence from behind the screen.

Ibrahim had the face of his daughter's murderer and on the recording was the voice of the officer who had covered for her lover Madeleine Wilson. He had no way of identifying them but fate was with him.

He returned from his meeting with General Xi to find Somchai Onruang had arranged an appointment with the representative of AGENDA. Suzy Webb, the face on his wife's phone, now transferred to a memory stick walked into his office. He had to fight to control his emotions as she sat before him discussing green energy issues. He just wanted to kill her. He resisted. He needed more. He wanted the identity of the person who had covered for her.

Somchai provided the solution in the form of a prostitute that set Suzy up to be abducted. They soon had Madeleine's name and Ibrahim took pleasure in killing Suzy himself. He gave Reza the name he had so long waited to hear. The new target for the drone strike would be the acting head of MI5. He liked the fact that she would be killed by drone shrike as many Jihadi leaders had been targeted and assassinated by the West in the same manner.

It was all in place. Then the Chinese came looking for their drone. Their link was Somchai Onruang. He had outlived his usefulness and needed to die before the Chinese or MI5 got to him. Ibrahim had his tip-off from the Policemen in his pay. He had him killed and he thought he was clear. The link to him and Dawar was severed with Somchai death.

He had not counted on Tim Burr. He had not counted on Tim and Harriet making the link back to Dawar and digging enough to figure out his connection to his daughter and Reza.

He had not conceived of Tim and David Chan cooperating in his abduction. Ibrahim tried to resist the torture but he broke as all men do. He gave up General Xi before he died. General Xi gave up the location of the drone at Inglewood Aviation without torture. He was going to die and felt no need to make it more painful than needs be.

The Chinese with Tim's sanction removed the threat of the drone by killing the pilots and blowing it up. All that remained was dealing with Reza, Ibrahim's nephew.

Reza now isolated decided on his suicide mission that culminated in the assault on the steps of the Mansion House. The dying throws of years of hate were played out in London all those years later. Reza killed and maimed before he too was shot by Philip. His target walked away unscathed and now sat in Tim's office in Thames House.

Tim sat with his head bowed next to Madeleine on the sofa. "That one decision to protect your lover, Suzy all those years ago has led to this," he said.

"It was love but after it weighed upon us. It was a chain dragging us apart. It snapped and the love was gone. There was no going back."

"It is time to face the consequences."

He walked to the door and the allowed the two uniformed officers into the room. "Madeleine Wilson I am arresting you for the aiding and abetting the murder of Javeria Kathia and perverting the course of justice." The police escorted her from Tim's office.

Alone and with tears in his eyes, he sat at his desk and taking pen and paper he began to write.

"Dear Mrs and Mrs Shaw,

It is with great personal sadness and loss that I write to offer my condolences on the death of you daughter Harriet ….."

Sufferance

Nicholas E Watkins

Jade

Copyright © Nicholas E Watkins 2018

Chapter 1

1899

The night sky lit up with the muzzle flash. Arthur was caught out in the open. It was clear that the Boers, Nicholas Van Leeuwen, his two cousins and their father were no fools and had kept watch on the infantry men trapped below them. Three of the Van Leeuwens had fought in the First Boer War and were well versed in the guerrilla tactics needed to give the British a bloody nose. Nicholas was a green horn, having only been in South Africa a few months. His uncle and cousins had grown up in the saddle and knew their Country well.

Nicholas had been put on watch and his keen eyes had spotted the movement in the darkness as Arthur had crawled from cover on his mission to fetch relief for his trapped comrades. The shot missed and Arthur got from his belly and ran. Had one of the other Boers spotted him, the outcome could have been different. Nicholas had been brought up in Rotterdam where there was no need to learn to shoot. His Uncle Joop and cousins, Jon and Andro had been taught to shoot as soon as they could hold a rifle. They would not have missed.

Merryweather saw the muzzle flash and he could shoot as well as any man. He had a natural ability that defied logic. His brain seemed to be able to pick up a target, static or moving and instinctively fire and hit with ease. The returned shot missed Nicholas's head by a matter of inches. He had readjusted his position for his second shot and that slight movement saved his life. He ducked back behind the rocks and realised that, if and when he fired again, a bullet would be returned instantly with deadly accuracy.

"What goes on?" his uncle appeared next to him

"One of the soldier boys is making a break for it."

"Where is he?"

"He has run for cover and is behind the ox cart," said Nicholas.

Joop moved a few feet away from where Nicholas had been firing and popped his head up from behind the rocks and shrub. "I see him," he said. "Does he have a gun? I don't see a rifle?"

"I didn't see one," said Nicholas.

"He's the kid," said Jon who had joined them along with his brother Andro. "He is still wet behind the ears. I am guessing they lightened his load as much as they could by dumping his kit and gun, so he could run for help."

"There is a detachment of mounted infantryman about six miles in that direction I reckon" said Andro. "We skirted round them yesterday. We don't want to be here if they turn up."

"No, you are right there. We need to make our way and join with the rest of the Boers."

"Are you just going to let them escape?" asked Nicholas almost incensed at the lack of commitment.

"What do you suggest? As our most experienced fighter who has been here for five minutes. You couldn't hit a barn door, with cannon from ten feet." Joop asked condescendingly.

Nicholas was young, barely seventeen and hot headed. He felt his face colour and his anger rise. His cousins just laughed. "I'll show you how it's done. He jumped to his feet and stormed to the horses.

"Come on, calm down. We were joking," called Jon. Nicholas was not listening. He was going to show them and prove a point. Jon rose to follow. The bullet missed him, but was too close for comfort.

"Keep your head down, if you want to keep it. That soldier boy down there can shoot," said Joop as he pulled his son back.

"Good damn it," said Andro. Nicholas jumped into the saddle and was galloping down towards the ox cart.

"Stupid bastard," said Joop. "Cover him, keep firing at their position."

"Jesus, what the hell is happening? Have you annoyed them or something?" said Sergeant Major Davies. The Boers were firing round after round at the group of infantrymen. Little flashes sprung from the rocks as the bullets ricocheted off them. It was like a sudden hail storm of lead. They all crouched lower as the firing continued.

"Well, they certainly are not short of ammo," said Corporal Manning.

Merryweather was and needed to pick his shots wisely. Given a larger supply of ammunition, they could all have laid down a barrage of covering fire for Arthur as he attempted to run for help. They could do little to aid their drummer boy trapped behind the cart.

"What's that?"

"Shit, shit, shit it's a horse. They have mounted up. They are going to run the poor lad down."

Merryweather tried to get a view over the boulder from where he had been hiding. No sooner had his head appeared than a shot was fired that narrowly missed him. He ducked back down.

The drumming of the horses' hooves grew louder as Nicholas galloped towards the cart where Arthur had taken cover. The carcases of the dead oxen had already begun to petrify and the sweet sickly smell of decay was making him feel ill as he hid behind the upturned wagon.

Arthur realised that he was in real trouble. He had barely made it three hundred yards before the shot had split the night sky. He knew that his comrades were doing their best to cover him but they were outgunned and the Boers had the advantage of their horses. He could not outrun a horse. He especially could not outrun a horse with an experienced rifleman in the saddle, who could shoot from the horses back.

Arthur was unarmed apart from his bayonet. He knew that even if he had his Lee Martin rifle, he was a pretty poor shot. To hit a rider at full gallop was no mean feat. He was trained to work as part of a unit firing volleys and advancing in strict order. He was no marksmen.

Their lack of ammunition and the position of the rest of the detail meant that they could do little to help him. Arthur realised he was on his own. He had to rely on himself. In that moment he became a man and a true soldier. He was young. He was strong. He had been trained to fight. He had been in battle only two days previously and he knew that overcoming fear was the key to survival. "Come and get it," he said out loud as he stepped out to face the oncoming horseman.

He thought of home. He thought of his father who he had no love for. Then he thought of Mabel Nicols. He, in that instant, realised that she had always been there in his mind. She was the one. "Come on, come and get it," he said again. "A bit late now to realise you love her."

Nicholas was in a veil of red mist. Burning from the taunts levelled at him by his cousins. Anger does not aid in judgement. He was pumped up, fuelled by rage and the need to prove himself. He was not a great rider. He was not a great shot. He was an angry, foolish, young boy whose testosterone had the better of him. He was galloping at full tilt, driving his horse on. His focussed on the cart. The horse was not a war horse. It was trained to hunt and herd. Bullets and charging at carts was new to it. The inexperience of the rider was not helping. The message coming through the legs and reigns were confusing. The cart loomed larger before them.

It was dark and the ground uneven. Nicholas pulled his rifle up to shoot at the defenceless soldier, dressed only in his underwear. He had no gun. He stood still with only a knife or something in his hand. Nicholas's confidence grew as he continued to ride down the man before him. He put the reigns in his mouth and levelled the rifle. It was stupid. He had seen Andro do it. Showing off and hitting a target on the farm. A trick shot, something Annie Oakley might do.

The horse was running free. Whereas Andro had years of riding experience and could control his horse using his legs, Nicholas had none of those skills. The horse saw the man standing still before them. If he continued, he would crash into him. It had not been trained to trample on people. In fact, its instinct was to avoid it. The lack of rider input, due to Nicholas's lack of ability, meant that the decision was left to the horse to make.

Arthur was not as intimidated by horse and rider as most. Growing up in Chipping Sodbury, he was used to horses and like most of the kids had learnt to ride. The horses were more fell and cart than hunter but he was familiar with them. He saw Nicholas pull up his rifle and level it at him. He held his ground. He knew that shooting from a galloping horse was possible. He had seen it at the Wild West Show back in Bristol, as a child, but he was also confident that hitting a target with any accuracy was not so likely.

He stood his ground. He had no choice. He had no gun. If he had, then he could have knelt, taken aim and fired at the rapidly approaching rider. He had a razor sharp bayonet and that was all. He would wait, dodge and attempt to stab rider or horse. He was calm, the calm of a focussed mind, the calm that comes before death or a battle. He had no other options so he stood and waited.

The horse was not so confident. It stopped and reared up. Its rider was concentrating, in his rage, on the kill and all semblance of horsemanship had been forgotten. Given a free hand, the horse was having none of it. Rider and horse crashed into the upturned cart as it tried to avoid trampling the man stood in its path.

Nicholas was taken by surprise. He was thrown from the horse as it collided with the cart. The wind was knocked from his lungs as he smashed into the ground. In an attempt to avoid hurting himself, he dropped the rifle and put out his hands to break his fall. He sprawled in a tangled mess at Arthur's feet.

Arthur saw the dazed boy, no older than himself, looking up at him. There was no hesitation, no pity, his training took over. The bayonet did what it was designed to do and Nicholas died quickly. He had acted on instinct and training. It would haunt him for the rest of his life. He would never forget the look of surprise on Nicholas's face as he died.

Arthur stood trembling, fixed to the spot. Suddenly he vomited.

The combination of fear and adrenaline was responsible. He was dazed. He was elated to be alive but also shocked and horrified. Mechanically, he pulled his bayonet out and wiped it on the boy's clothing. The horse stood, unmoved nibbling at some grass, its body bathed in sweat.

"Get out of there," Arthur became aware at the Colour shouting at him.

Joop, Andro and Jon had mounted their horses and were riding down on him. Merryweather had only three rounds left and could do little. Nicholas's family, sensing that the infantry men had little ammunition left, were going to try and finish matters or at least recover the body.

Arthur recovered his composure. He approached Nicholas's horse as calmly as he could, talking gently to it. He gathered the reigns and pulled himself into the saddle. The saddle was wider and had a higher back than he was used to. He kicked the horse into life and galloped from the scene.

Looking back, he could see that the three Boers had taken up position behind the cart and again had Davies, Merryweather, Sweet and Manning pinned down. Arthur knew that they could not last long. He rode and hoped.

Chapter 2

1891

The streets of Chipping Sodbury were packed with families making their way to church. The men were in their Sunday best. The labourers and the less well off washed and shaved and put on clean shirts and had their trousers washed and pressed. Their wives would try and put on an appearance of elegance in their, often thread bear, frocks. Efforts were made with headgear by the women, their bonnets and hats had been decorated with some flowers from the fields and gardens. It was September and the village was still in bloom.

Mary White was also dressed in her Sunday best and held her Mother's hand as they joined the procession to St. Johns. Her grandfather walked ahead, talking to the other men in the village. She saw Mr and Mrs Harris and their three children making their way to Service He was the local solicitor and the brass plaque hung on the wall of his office, next to the Portcullis Public House. It was a standing joke that he was ideally placed to find clients for his services.

The Harris's were well respected in the Village, the men doffed their caps and the women almost curtsied as they passed the Solicitor and his family. Their clothing alone put them apart in status. Mr Harris dressed, as though he was about to appear in court, in total elegance in contrast to the hob nailed booted men, who worked the fields. His wife's Sunday bonnet and coat made her the envy of the other women. Mary herself envied the beautiful dress and soft buttoned shoes worn by their eldest daughter. Mary felt her own drabness and lack of worth as she watched the Harris's join the procession to the Church.

The benches in the church were not comfortable. The pews seemed to have been engineered to cause the maximum discomfort to the bum as the Vicar indulged himself in a long winded sermon that seemed to last longer than the Forty Days and Forty Nights the Lord actually spent in the Wilderness.

Finally, the lesson stopped and the Vicar stepped down from the lectern and took up his position at the head of the congregation for a bit of praying and the hymns. While they knelt and prayed, Mary took the opportunity to look around. She caught sight of Mabel, who smiled back at her. She wiggled her fingers, unfurling them from their clasped position held for prayer.

Mabel Nicols was her friend. They sat together in class in the cottage school and now, after Sunday school, they would sit and talk on their way home. Mabel had a mother and father and lived in a tiny cottage opposite the old village pump. Her father was a farm labourer and her mother worked, cleaning for the Harris family.

Mabel's father was a keen patron of the Portcullis. He was not a bad man, better than most. Land work was hard, poorly paid and dangerous. Jobs were going as the steam engine took the work from the horse and the man. Industrialisation was on the way, but moving slowly in the countryside, so there were still jobs for the healthy and strong on the farms.

It was September and the harvest was a time for all to look forward to. The work was hard and the pay poor but it was a change from the humdrum drab of the everyday. It was still a time for cart rides for all, old and young alike, to gather in the crop. They worked from sunrise to sunset. Stopping and picnicking in the fields on the food brought by the farmer's wives for those helping gather in the crop. To Mabel it was freedom.

Mabel's mother was wearing a veil of black lace, covering the top half of her face. Mary and everyone else knew that Mr Nicols had clearly extended his stay at the bar in the Portcullis. He rarely got drunk compared to many in the town, but when he did, the outcome would be inevitable. It was not uncommon to beat your wife and it was a husband's right as head of the family to keep the women in their place. Mrs Nicols knew it was her fault. She could not help but nag. This frustration of seeing her husband spend his wages in the pub made her reckless and she could not hold her tongue. Her husband was not the type of man to take orders from a woman. If she overstepped the mark, she knew the consequences. Domestics, as they were called, were not a matter the police wanted to get involved in. What went on between man and wife was between them and God. The man was the man and it was his role to keep his wife in check and give his children a good beating when they deserved it.

The sun was out and the weather hot, the meadow in bloom. It was a beautiful day and Mabel and Mary sat with their shoes off, making daisy chains. The class had been taken by Mrs Hewitt, the Vicar's wife, that Sunday. When the Vicar took the class it was boring to the extent of torture. His wife had a cheerful disposition and, unlike her husband, held up her religion with a certain amount of joy and hope. The Vicar was grounded in the fire, brimstone and puritanical end of the Bible, old school, Old Testament and as miserable as a castrated bull as Mabel would say.

"Are you excited?" asked Mabel.

"About what?"

"The Wild West show?"

"Buffalo Bill and the Rough Riders, it sounds so exciting. I am not sure if we will have the money though." said Mary.

"Mother has been putting a bit away as soon as the posters went up, so I think so, unless Father finds it and spends it in the Portcullis. Don't worry. I am sure we will be there. It will be the event of the century," said Mabel.

They were interrupted by the sound of swearing and shouting. A group of boys were involved in an argument by the stile that led to the meadow from the lane.

"It's the Watt's boys again," said Mabel.

The ginger one and the one with the black hair?"

"That's them."

"They seem to be in a fight with about, four other lads."

"And they're winning by the looks of it."

Edward and Arthur Watts were known in Chipping Sodbury as tearaways. Their father was as hard as nails and everyone avoided crossing him. He had brought the boys up tough, never sparing the rod. Arthur, with his red hair, was eight but looked older and was as strong as an ox, with a bull neck. Edward was a year younger and was not so inclined to anger but when roused, he was ferocious. He would go red and any potential opponent would think him fearful. That was an error, after red came white and a trembling throughout his body, an adrenaline rush before he exploded into violence.

Edward was kind, thoughtful and never sought conflict but a demon raged in him when he felt an injustice had been served. Arthur was strong and enjoyed conflict and violence, a tough little man. Their Father was incapable of showing affection and preferred to use the back of his hand when dealing with his sons, rather than talk to them. Edward feared their father, but knew it was wrong to disrespect him. Arthur hated him and was reaching the point where he wanted to fight back. The conflict between Father and son was building.

"They're a nightmare." said Mary.

"But the ginger one's not bad looking." said Mabel.

"What would Mrs Hewitt say, you looking at the boys?"

The two girls made their way from the fields back towards the high street. The stall and tables, from the Mop held the previous few days, was being tidied away and carts were being loaded. The Mop had been held twice yearly since medieval times. Employers would come to the town looking for workers. No one quite knew why it was called the Mop. The folk law was that the workers would carry the tools of their trade to advertise their labour. Carpenters would carry a saw, masons a chisel and domestics a mop, hence the name. Most of the work in the area was quarrying, coal mining, farming and domestic service.

The posters for the Wild West show were plastered around the High Street. "A shilling entrance, that's a lot." said Mary. Her father had died or disappeared and she had never known him. Her mother worked cleaning and her grandfather wove cloth at home for the hat trade. They lived in a small leaky cottage in Hatters Lane. Money was tight and her grandfather was old and was earning less each year.

"They have laid on special carts to take people to the railway station at Yate," said Mabel.

"I've never been on a train. That would truly be an adventure."

Chapter 3

It was the afternoon session and the onlookers had settled in around the ground. The weather had stayed fine and the Chipping Sodbury eleven were getting ready to bat. There was a loud round of applause as the batsmen made their way onto the pitch. There was an air of expectancy as they approached the crease.

Mabel and Mary were sat in the shade of the trees where they could get a good view of the pitch and the pavilion, in front of which sat the great and the good of the village. The Harris's, Mr Pratt, the governor of the workhouse and his wife were there, as well as Doctor Grace. The doctor was there to watch his son bat.

Alfred Grace was captaining the Chipping Sodbury side. There had been a rumour that his brother, W. G., the most famous cricketer in the country, might put in an appearance. His season in first class cricket had been cut short owing to a knee injury. The spectators were out of luck. W. G., as he was commonly called, was there but sat watching with his Father, resting his recalcitrant leg. His bother, however, was a mean batsman in his own right, having appeared for Gloucester on a number of occasions and still playing in the colts.

"Pay attention," Edward and Arthur Watts received a warning

from the scorer. The boys had the task of putting the score on the big black board. In front of them they had a white pile of numbers. "If you mess it up, I shall speak to your father and see you have a good hiding."

The boys had been roped into scoring in a bid to stop them creating some mischief or other. Under the eye of the scorer and his assistant, there was a vain hope that some form of stupidity or unruliness that might interrupt the afternoon's proceedings could be avoided

The match got underway and, for the most part the boys behaved themselves. In a pause in play between overs, while the fielders readjusted their positions, the boys scanned the crowd.

"Do you see that girl with the blonde hair?" said Arthur.

"Where?"

"There, under the trees,"

"I think the one next to her is prettier?"

"Definitely not, I prefer a blonde."

"I like the look of black hair and dark eyes, it is exotic. That's what it is," said Edward.

"Exotic," scoffed Arthur, "You read too many books."

"At least I can read."

"I can read, are you saying I am stupid?" Arthur was getting riled.

"No, just ginger and ugly," laughed Edward, provoking his

brother.

Arthur was about to indulge in a bit of fratricide to alleviate the tedium of updating the scoreboard when there was the sound of a loud whack. "Pack it in you two," said the scorer, having clipped Arthur round the ear.

"That hurt," said Arthur.

"It'll hurt more if I take that bat over there and apply it to your backside. Now stop playing silly buggers, the next over is starting. Pay attention."

The two boys reluctantly set themselves to the task in hand.

"The ginger one just got a clip round the ear," said Mabel.

"I didn't notice." said Mary.

"You did so. You like him don't you? Admit it!"

"No I do not. How dare you Mabel Nicols, how dare you say such a thing."

"So it's true then." she laughed.

Mary turned a little red-faced. "Well just a bit, perhaps. Anyway you like his brother Edward."

"Well perhaps, just a little bit," she mimicked her friend. They both fell into a fit of the giggles.

There was a round of applause as the cricket ball sped past the two girls. Dr Grace had just hit a boundary. Mabel stood up, chased the ball and threw it back to the fielder. She sat down. "Well at least that was something to do."

"Cricket has to be the most boring thing ever invented. I do not have the faintest idea what is happening and it seems to go on forever. Look at the scoreboard, what do you think it means, who is wining?"

"I don't know and I don't care."

There was a gasp from the crowd as Alfred Grace was caught in the slips from a fine edge. There was a round of applause as he walked and made his way to the pavilion. The crowd stood as he raised his bat to acknowledge their support. His father stood and shook his son's hand. Mr Harris patted him on his back as he made his way into the clubhouse. The next batsman appeared and the applause restarted to greet him as he made his way to the crease and took guard. The two girls sat down and resumed their conversation. The two boys resigned themselves to several more hours of tedium until the game finished.

Finally, as the light faded, the game was over and Chipping Sodbury had achieved a rare win, helped by the forty eight runs added by their captain and local doctor. Mabel and Mary hugged by way of parting and went their separate ways.

Edward and Arthur arrived home to find their father asleep and snoring loudly in his chair in the downstairs room. Their mother put her fingers to her lips, urging silence. She ushered them past their father into the scullery. They were not normally the quiet types but when he was sleeping with a belly full of cider, they had learned that it was best to let the sleeping dog lay. If he slept through the night, he would leave the house at dawn and head to the farm. He would be bad tempered with a raging head and a dry mouth but he would be away from the home.

Waking him from his slumber prematurely would be like poking a snake with a stick. With no means of drinking further on a Sunday, he would be in a dangerous mood. Rage was never far from his persona but with the drink it was certain. The usual recipient of the man's temper would be Arthur and if he was unavailable, it would be their mother. Having relieved themselves in the outhouse, they crept their way up the tiny, twisting stairs that led directly from the room downstairs, through a door leading to the loft where they all slept. They succeeded in not waking their father as they crept into bed. Their parents slept further along, in an area which had been partitioned off.

"Good night boys." she whispered as she closed the door that divided the sleeping quarters. For once, Arthur and Edward knew the importance of silence and stayed their natural temperaments.

In the cottage Mary shared with her Mother and grandfather, she got into bed with her mother. It was nine o'clock and they would be up at five. Mary knew her mother was getting tired and had pain in her stomach. She would sleep fitfully and wake still tired. She should see the doctor but doctors cost money and they had little. Her grandfather was getting slower and slower and hardly brought in any money. He was getting forgetful and wandered off sometimes. She would have to go and find him.

13071920R00118

Printed in Great Britain
by Amazon